▼  ▼  ▼  ▼  ▼

In the confusion, the frightening old man suddenly lashed out and grabbed Rachel by the straps of her backpack. She found herself staring into the clouded eyes of blind Old Tuz, close enough to count every yellow tooth and gray hair. The amulet and its chicken scratchings swung from his neck like a pendulum above her forehead. Old Tuz's weathered face grew frenzied and urgent.

"*Var,*" he whispered softly, so that only Rachel could hear. "I have seen it. It is there, on the mountain that burns within."

Join Rachel and Elliot on all
their adventures!

**TRUTHQUEST**

*The Mountain That Burns Within*
*Valley of the Giant*
*Treasure of the Hidden Tomb*

# The Mountain That Burns Within

## Tad Hardy

ChariotVICTOR
PUBLISHING
A Division of Cook Communications

Chariot Books is an imprint of ChariotVictor Publishing
Cook Communications, Colorado Springs, CO 80918
Cook Communications, Paris, Ontario
Kingsway Communications, Eastbourne, England

THE MOUNTAIN THAT BURNS WITHIN
© 1997 by Tad Hardy

ISBN 0-7814-30011
Designed by Andrea Boven
Cover illustration by John Lytle
Map illustration by Guy Wolek
First printing, 1997
Printed in the United States of America
01  00  99  98  97      5  4  3  2  1

*For Mom and Dad,*
*who have always loved by example*

▲　　▲　　▲　　▲　　▲

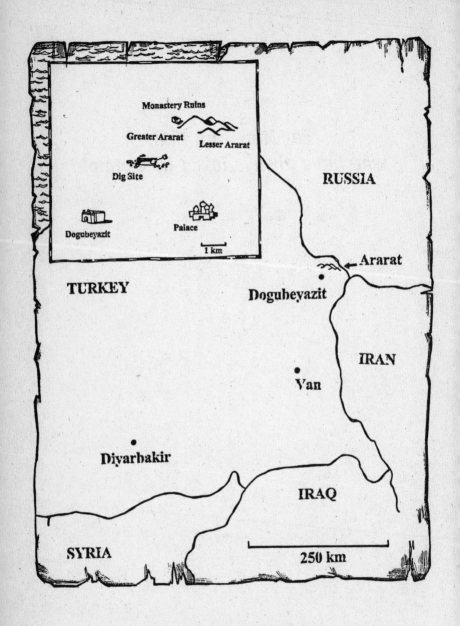

# People and Places in Turkey

**Anatolian** (an-a-TO-lee-un)  A large sheepdog found in eastern Turkey

**Apo** (AH-po) Uncle

**Armut** (ahr-MOOT)  Uncle Mason's friend

**Diyarbakir** (dee-YAHR-bah-kuhr)  A city in eastern Turkey

**Dogubeyazit** (doh-OO-bey-yah-zuht)  A village near the dig site

**Effendi** (eh-FEN-dee)  A term of respect, like "sir"

**Mehlat** (may-LOT)  The pilot of the plane from Diyarbakir to Dogubeyazit

**Selik** (SEH-lik)  A shepherd friend of Armut

**Tuz** (TOOZ)  An old man in Dogubeyazit

**yaila** (YAY-la)  A small, shepherd village made up of tents

**Yedi** (ya-DEE)  Armut's nephew and Rachel and Elliot's friend

# CHAPTER 1

Rachel could hardly believe her eyes.

There before her, half-buried in a thin layer of golden sand, lay an honest-to-goodness, real-live skeleton. A human skeleton, so close she could reach out and touch it. The lower leg bones were topped by kneecaps shaped like skipping stones; the long upper leg bones twisted their way into the cradle-shaped hip. Her eyes followed the gently curving spine through its ribcage to the flattened shoulder blades, poking from the sand like two pieces of a broken china plate. One arm, bent at the elbow, protected the yellowed ribs. And at the tip of the twisted forearm rested a handful of short, bony fingers, one wearing a golden ring band nearly hidden by an ocean-blue gemstone bigger than Rachel's thumb.

At the spine's tip lay a chalk-colored skull with its jaws slightly open. Rachel's eyes were drawn to its hollow eye sockets staring back at her blankly. They seemed to reach out to her, yearning to reveal a hundred hidden secrets.

Lost in thought, she hardly noticed the low humming sound that began to vibrate beneath the dry sand. Suddenly, a faint blue glow flickered for an instant behind the skull's empty eyes. Then it was gone. Rachel felt a shiver race through her body as she instinctively jumped back a step. Then her heart pounded into her throat as the blue glow reappeared, growing brighter and brighter. Tiny ringlets of sand rippled and danced at the edges of the bones. The hum grew louder.

Bravely, Rachel nudged herself closer to the humming skeleton. She reached out a trembling hand toward the sand.

"That's a good way to get the daylights shocked out of you, Rachel," said a voice behind her. Rachel whirled on her heels and came eyeball-to-eyeball with her cousin, Elliot.

"There's a problem with the wiring," he continued. "That's why Dad brought that display case back here to storage. Once it's repaired, we'll return it to the main floor of the museum. In the meantime, I would advise you not to touch it."

"I had no intention of touching anything," Rachel said as calmly as she could, her heart still pounding.

"Right. I suppose you were just waving at your reflection in the glass cover."

"Well, it could use a good wiping down. Just look at all this dirt." She blew across the top of the glass case and feigned a cough at the small cloud of sandy dust rising into the air.

"There's supposed to be dirt, Rachel. After all, this

used to be part of a tomb." Elliot stepped behind the
display case and unplugged the electric cord. The
humming sound faded away, taking the dim blue light
with it.

After clearing a space among stacks of books and
field equipment, Elliot hopped onto one of the heavy
black lab tables cluttering the museum storage room.
He began thumbing through a large picture book with
a frowning Indian chief on the cover.

"How long has he been lying there like that?" Rachel
wondered, still staring at the skeleton. She almost
hoped Elliot wouldn't answer.

"I'm not certain, actually. Probably a thousand years
or so, give or take a hundred."

"No, I mean, how long has he been lying here, in this
glass box?"

"Oh. Not long," Elliot replied, barely looking up from
the oversized pages of the book propped against his
knees. "Dad brought him back from the expedition
this spring. And him, and him, and her," he added.

With each "him" and "her" Elliot pointed to separate
cardboard boxes, stacked neatly on pallets at one end
of the storage room. A long series of numbers had
been written hastily in Magic Marker on the side of
each box. Below the numbers was a blue circle surrounding the image of a cracked clay pot with handles
on each side. Next to the pot were the letters
"S.I.M.A."

Rachel noticed that every box in the room had the
same clay pot stencil and every box read "S.I.M.A." So
did the handle of every pickax and hand trowel and

hammer and chisel strewn around the room. It was also written on all the book covers, notebooks, and wooden shelves lining the painted brick walls.

"By the way—you don't call this a glass box, Rachel," Elliot said, correcting her. "It's a display case. There's a big difference, you know."

"I doubt that it makes much difference to him . . . or her or . . . whatever," Rachel said, pointing to the silent skeleton. "Yuk."

"Don't you have museums in Kentucky?" Elliot asked.

"Bunches and bunches of them. You know that."

"Do you ever visit them?"

"Sure." Rachel knew her answer didn't sound so sure. She ignored Elliot, busying herself with writing her name on the dusty case with her finger. Elliot looked at her with his head cocked to one side, waiting for a better answer. So Rachel gave him one.

"Well, sometimes I visit the museums."

He laid his book aside and crossed his arms, waiting. He knew her well, almost too well, considering Rachel and her mother had moved to Kentucky from Great Britain just a year ago. Visiting relatives was not high on her mother's list of priorities, although Rachel would now see more of Elliot and Uncle Mason since they lived in nearby Indiana, only a few hours away. Maybe it was because they were cousins, or because their birthdays were only a week apart—whatever the reason, Elliot always seemed to know when Rachel was covering up. *Not lying,* she thought to herself, *just covering up.*

"Okay," Rachel finally conceded. "Once. I went to a museum once, with my friend and her mom when we lived in England. But it was an art museum, not a creepy museum with bones in boxes."

Smiling, Elliot uncrossed his arms and adjusted the gold-rimmed glasses resting on his nose.

"These skeletons are from a permanent dig site over near Evansville. A place called Angel Mounds. Dad goes there every spring to work. Here, look."

He opened his book to a colored drawing of Indians wrapped in blankets huddled around a campfire. Behind them, in the evening shadows, stood rows of long wooden houses and low sloping mounds shaped like camel humps.

"Angel Mounds used to look something like this, back when Indians lived there. At least that's what Dad says. See these dirt mounds? They're actually burial tombs. But Angel Mounds doesn't look anything like this anymore."

Rachel put the finishing touches on her name, written in cursive on the dusty display case.

"How do you know?" she asked.

"I went there a few months ago. The museum sponsored a teaching expedition for some of the archeology students at the university. Dad figured I was old enough to tag along and help catalog artifacts. Some dig sites don't allow kids, at least not the sites where artifacts are collected as museum specimens. But I suppose everyone thought I was older than twelve."

"I suppose everyone knew Uncle Mason was your father, besides being the teacher, so they didn't dare say a word," Rachel shot back.

Elliot calmly ignored her remark. "We learned a lot about archeology. You know what we learned first?"

"What?"

"We learned never to touch a display case with faulty wiring."

"Funny, Elliot." Rachel didn't appreciate the smirk on his face. "Although I doubt all of these Sima Indians lying about find that remark humorous."

"All of these *what*?" Elliot seemed puzzled.

"These Sima Indians, or what's left of them." Rachel swept an open hand around the storage room dramatically. "I don't hear any of them laughing, do you?"

Elliot rolled his eyes. "SIMA isn't an Indian tribe, Rachel. It's an acronym—when you make a word using the first letter of a group of words. SIMA stands for Southern Indiana Museum of Archeology—S.I.M.A. That's why everything here is stamped with that blue clay pot. These artifacts belong to the museum." He swept his hand in a wide circle, imitating Rachel. "I keep forgetting you've never been here before. Let me make the proper introductions. Rachel Ashton, meet SIMA. SIMA, this is Rachel, Archeologist Extraordinaire."

"And this is Elliot Conner," she announced to the storage room walls, playing up her natural British accent and taking an especially arrogant tone, "Director of Glass Box Fixing, and general Pain in the Neck."

Elliot hopped from his tabletop perch. "Let's go see the museum workroom. It's awesome."

"So are snakes," muttered Rachel. "But I'd rather not *see* one."

He led her from the windowless storage room through a short hallway. It opened into a room that had a long row of windows along one wall. This room felt light and airy, yet it surrounded them with pungent smells—musty soil, rusting metal, vinegar. Workbenches and short stools lined the walls. Thin sheets of plywood lay across several of the bench tops. A crusty metal sink hung precariously from a pair of old wall brackets in one corner of the room. Beneath it, a shallow puddle of water grew steadily larger with every drip from the leaky drainpipes above it.

"This is the workroom," Elliot explained. "It doesn't always look this messy. . . . Sometimes it looks worse."

Rachel couldn't imagine it looking any messier. Junk was stashed everywhere. Slowly she surveyed the room: small shovels with hinged handles, a pickax caked in mud, pruning shears, gloves, goggles, tweezers, wire, rope, cloth bags, paper bags, a tape measure, massive rolls of cotton, even an old toothbrush. Dirt-clod trails crisscrossed the floor, leading toward the corners of the room. At the end of each trail stood bundles of rolled paper maps stuffed into long brown tubes, like cornstalks waiting for harvest. The countertops overflowed with tin trays and cardboard boxes crammed full of glass bottles. Bone fragments mingled with pieces of stone, and pottery lay scattered among microscopes resting atop lighted worktables. A large green travel trunk sat squarely in the center of the floor. Its lid was propped open with a clipboard.

"Are you sure this isn't the *junk* room?"

"Positive," Elliot said. "I've spent most of my summer

here, learning to restore artifacts. Pottery, wood, stuff like that."

"Lucky you," Rachel said sarcastically. She had to admit, though, the place had a certain charm. For one thing, the clutter reminded her a little of her own room back in Kentucky, except for the dirt. She was sure her mother would agree. But she also felt a sense of anticipation in the room, as if great discoveries and ideas were brought here from all over the world.

"Dad carries most of this equipment with him to dig sites." Elliot nodded toward the open trunk. "But if it won't fit in there, it doesn't go. Right now, he's packing for his annual trip to Turkey."

"Oh, Turkey. Turkey is wonderful. I love Turkey." Rachel hastily showed interest in Elliot's comments, hoping he wouldn't notice that she had accidentally fidgeted the knob off one of the microscopes.

"Really? What do you know about Turkey?" Elliot asked.

"Well, it's quite tasty if you stuff it with dressing and dab on a little cranberry sauce." She couldn't help herself. She burst out laughing.

"Laugh all you want, Rachel. But Dad leaves next week to spend nine days at the Urartian digs in eastern Turkey. And I'm going with him."

"How perfectly grand!" she exclaimed. "Just what I've always dreamed of doing—digging through rotten old tombs on my hands and knees all day, dusting off bones, gluing teeny tiny pieces of busted clay pots back together out in the middle of nowhere . . . it sounds lovely."

Rachel sauntered away from the microscopes and lifted Uncle Mason's safari hat from a coat hook near the door. The hat practically swallowed her head when she slipped it on. She leaned over and pretended to search for invisible artifacts, pacing back and forth, shading her eyes from a blazing, make-believe sun.

"I can already hear your back-to-school report. 'How I Spent My Summer Vacation, Picking Over Old Bones at the Martian Digs.'" Rachel noticed Elliot smiling to himself. "What are you grinning at?" she asked.

"I'm glad to hear you're excited about the digs, Rachel." His smile grew wider. "Because you're going with us."

CHAPTER 2

"We're flying in that?" Rachel stammered in disbelief.

Elliot raised the brim of his hat, opened a sleepy eye, and squinted out the giant, tinted window of the airport terminal. But he didn't answer. Fifteen feet below on the tarmac sat a bulky metal machine that, with a little imagination, looked something like an airplane.

Stubbornly, Rachel pressed her nose to the window and stared hard at her first Turkish sunrise. The colors poured over the distant mountains and spilled across the runways of Diyarbakir Airport. This plane was much smaller than the jets that had carried them all the way from Indianapolis. Much smaller. It wouldn't have polite flight attendants serving up soft drinks and peanuts as did the flight from Indiana to New York. The seats wouldn't recline like those in the jumbo jet that carried her, Elliot, and Uncle Mason to London in the pitch-black darkness. And no one would offer to fluff her pillow or get an extra blanket if she needed one, or tell silly jokes over the airplane's intercom system the way pilots and attendants had done from

London to Istanbul to here.

"I said, 'We're flying in *that*?'" Rachel repeated. This time she flipped up Elliot's hat herself, to get an answer.

"Yes, we're flying in that. All the way to Dogubeyazit."

He dropped the hat back over his eyes, settling deeper into the cracked leather seats lining the boarding area that had, for the past few hours, doubled as their sleeping quarters.

Rachel put her hands on her hips. "But it's practically an antique. Are you sure Uncle Mason didn't find it at some old dig? It has propellers."

"Two. I hope," Elliot mumbled. "But it can fly with just one if necessary."

"I don't care if it has five hundred propellers. I am *not* flying to Dog Biscuit in that thing." Rachel squeezed her hands into fists against her sides to show her determination.

"Sure you are. Unless you intend to walk for two solid weeks to get there," said Elliot.

"I never intended to get there in the first place," she muttered.

Elliot remained silent for a time before he answered.

"Look, Rachel. Neither of us has been to Turkey before. And you've never been on a real dig. Just think of this as an adventure."

"As if I need adventures," Rachel thought aloud, facing the window. "Living with Mother makes every day an adventure. I never know what to expect from one day to the next." She turned to face Elliot. "You know, she never told me I was coming with you and Uncle Mason. I guess it slipped her mind that her only daughter was shuttling off to the other side of the world to spend the last two weeks of summer in exile."

"Your mom isn't that bad," offered Elliot, lifting his hat. "A little scatterbrained, maybe, but not bad."

"That's easy for you to say. She's just your aunt. But she's *my* mother."

"She swore Dad and me to secrecy," Elliot explained. "Then we helped her make all of your travel arrangements through the museum. This trip was supposed to be a surprise."

"Believe me, it was a surprise," huffed Rachel. Deep down she appreciated Elliot's attempts to help her feel better. But she felt betrayed that her mother had made the decision without asking her first. She was old enough to make her own decisions.

"I gave up two weeks of tennis lessons to come here," she continued. "I can't even pronounce the name of this place. Everyone dresses funny and talks gibberish, and now we're sleeping on airport chairs, waiting to fly to another place I can't pronounce!" *Dogubeyazit.* She had heard Uncle Mason say the name a handful of times, but for Rachel it was simpler to call it Dog Biscuit. So she did.

She looked again at the airplane below them. Elliot was right, as usual. It had two propellers, one on each side of the fuselage. Behind the propellers, twisting, brown lightning bolts of oil streaked the wings—telltale signs of leaks from the old engines. The entire airplane had been painted beige except for one broad patch of sloppy green paint trimming the topside of the nose to cover obvious repairs.

Two men stood talking near the open door to the cockpit. Rachel guessed that the one wearing a flat beret and starched khaki shirt must be the pilot. His eyes were hidden behind a pair of sunglasses. But the other man intrigued her. He resembled the airplane beside him—old, worn, a little rough around the edges, with skin the color of sand. A real survivor. Mostly Rachel noticed his hands, which seemed to move in wide sweeps with each word spoken, and his odd clothes. Colorful designs danced up and down the long sleeves of his shirt. He wore a wide sash for a belt, and below it his pant legs hung baggy and crumpled, all the way to his ankles. They were so baggy that Rachel thought the light breeze might billow them like small sails and float him away. He seemed dressed for snowy winds, not for the waves of oppressive heat rising from the black tarmac.

Suddenly Uncle Mason's booming laugh caught Rachel's attention. He strode down the boarding area corridor with a cloth satchel over one shoulder, and a small basket of fruit tucked beneath his arm. His light-colored field clothes made Uncle Mason, a big, strapping man, look even bigger.

"Well, have you two caught up on your sleep?" he wondered.

"Almost," answered Elliot.

"No," Rachel said flatly.

Uncle Mason removed the satchel from his broad shoulder. "We'll be spending the night in Dogubeyazit. If we need any last-minute supplies, we can get them there. But at dawn, when we leave the city, we leave all the comforts of home. It will take most of tomorrow to caravan to the dig site and set up camp. And we'll each have jobs to do once we arrive."

He stepped toward Rachel, stroked his beard thoughtfully, then pointed over her shoulder toward the tarmac.

"Quite an aircraft, eh?" Uncle Mason grinned. "It's really quite safe, much safer than it looks." He winked a kind blue eye at her. "And don't let the props worry you. This old plane has battled its way through many a dust storm without so much as a sputter. Mehlat is a top-notch pilot."

Uncle Mason stood before the giant window and waved the fruit basket high above his head, catching the pilot's attention. Mehlat's sunglasses glanced up, and the mustached mouth below them smiled. With several hurried scoops of his arm, Mehlat gestured for them to come down. Then he slapped Mr. Baggy Pants soundly on the shoulder and shook his hand warmly.

Mehlat walked to the rear of the airplane where he helped another man, also in khakis, tug two SIMA travel trunks up a ramp and into the plane's belly, all under Uncle Mason's watchful eye.

"That's the last of our equipment," said Uncle Mason. He nudged Elliot and winked again at Rachel. "Okay you two, let's not keep Mehlat waiting. He can make a twin prop fly like an eagle, but I'm afraid he has the patience of a starving lion."

A narrow stairway led them from the boarding area down to the tarmac and the waiting airplane. Rachel felt as if she were about to enter a giant bucket. Inside, the plane was little more than a hollow shell—a big cargo area with one bench-type seat bolted to each side. *No need for seat assignments in this thing*, Rachel thought. *Just pick one, Bench One or Bench Two.*

As they entered the side door, Rachel was shocked to learn they were not alone. A middle-aged woman, flanked by two graying men, sat on the far bench facing the doorway. Both men were dressed like Mr. Baggy Pants. One wore a stocking cap. The woman shyly straightened her brightly colored skirt and tugged at a cloth covering draped across her hair.

No one had told Rachel there would be other passengers. It seemed no one bothered to tell her anything. She was tempted to snub them—she was good at being rude and she knew it. Instead she nodded at the Baggy Pants twins and offered a tight smile to the dark-eyed woman. The woman returned her smile, revealing big empty spaces where her teeth should have been.

Mehlat hurried them in. He closed the door behind Rachel and crawled through a narrow space connecting the cockpit with the cargo area. Rachel and Elliot grabbed seats on Bench Two. Uncle Mason sat in the copilot seat next to Mehlat, his radio headphones strapped across the top of his balding head. The engines cranked, sputtered, cranked again. Finally the right propeller powered up, droning away like a giant bumblebee. The left propeller soon followed. The entire airplane vibrated.

"So . . . how long does it take to fly to Dog Biscuit?" Rachel called out to Elliot above the engines' rattle.

He pointed to his ears and shook his head. Both props were turning fiercely now and the loud droning had become a roar. Apparently Elliot couldn't hear a thing she said. She unbuckled herself and slid closer to him.

"How long?" She yelled through cupped hands. "How long to Dog Biscuit?"

Elliot nodded. He retrieved a folded map from his shirt pocket and together they opened it onto the flat lid of one of the travel trunks. An outline of the country of Turkey lay before them—one end surrounded by seas and the other end speckled with shaded squiggles representing mountains. Hundreds of unfamiliar names cluttered the map.

Rachel drew her finger across the map until she found a circle labeled "Diyarbakir." Elliot nodded again and pointed to a small black dot about six inches to the northeast. Underneath the dot it read "Dogubeyazit." He measured the distance between the circle and the dot using his thumb and middle finger. Then he matched the distance to a scale mileage chart at the bottom of the map.

"About 500 kilometers!" he hollered holding up five fingers so Rachel could understand. Several seconds later he had finished the calculation in his head and this time he raised two fingers. "About two hours!"

Rachel couldn't hear his answer but she definitely could count fingers.

"Two hours!" she screamed above the propeller roar. "In this old chicken coop?"

Before Elliot could answer, the plane began to move.

Mehlat wasted little time, pulling the plane's wheels from the runway at the earliest possible moment. Rachel felt her stomach fill with butterflies and flop into her shoes. They were on their way.

Elliot remained buckled to the bench seat jutting from the side of the open cargo area, studying the map and rummaging through the travel trunk nearest them. The three extra passengers sat in silence, staring out the window at the blue-gray mountains and scrubby vegetation rolling by below. Occasionally the men exchanged glances or hollered briefly to one another over the engine roar. In gibberish.

Soon after they had cleared the first mountain range, Elliot tapped Rachel on the shoulder. He held up two empty tin cans connected by a length of string tied through a hole punched in the bottom of each can. He handed one can to Rachel and gestured for her to hold it to her ear. Then he held the other end to his lips and pulled the string taut. Moments later she heard his voice, loud and clear.

"Can you hear me?"

Rachel nodded.

"Are you having fun yet?"

Rachel shook her head.

"We made this tin-can telephone as part of a special project in science class last year. I knew it would come in handy."

Elliot placed his can to his ear. Now it was Rachel's turn to talk. She drew the can to her mouth and took a deep breath.

"I'm missing two weeks of tennis lessons!" she

yelled. She was in no mood to talk into a can for two hours.

Elliot cringed and jerked the can from his ear, nearly knocking his glasses from his nose. He set his jaw angrily and, after pointing at Rachel, he pointed to the side of his head and twisted his finger in a circle, over and over.

An hour and a half later the plane banked sharply to the north. Rachel fumbled for her seat belt. For a long moment she could see nothing but sky through the window. Then, as Mehlat piloted the plane level again, a tall spire came into view. It resembled a giant stack of red checkers topped by a gray cone pointing skyward. A tortoise shell dome of a building mushroomed from beneath the spire, casting its round shadow onto a maze of walled courtyards and dark archways. Rachel had visited castles before, in England, but had never seen one like this. This was the castle of a fairy-tale princess with towers and pillars and turrets and balconies, nestled like a tarnished jewel at the foot of the mountains.

Rachel poked Elliot's ribs and motioned to the tin-can telephone. Warily, he lifted it to his ear.

"What is that?" she asked into the can. She didn't yell this time. She held the can to her ear for his reply.

"It is the Saray," his voice buzzed. "The Palace of Kings and Beggars, just south of Dog Biscuit. I've read about it. The owner considered the palace the most beautiful in all the world.

"About two hundred years ago . . ."

Rachel pulled the can back to her lips. "I didn't ask

for a guided tour," she snapped, cutting Elliot short. "I just wondered what it was." Tired and cranky, she was in no mood to listen to Elliot's complete history of the place. She would see it for herself. After all, she had eight boring days to use up—she might as well spend one day exploring a fairy-tale palace.

Small pockets of hot air jostled the plane as it descended into Dogubeyazit minutes later. The palace dimmed behind clouds of dust from the runway. An instant later the plane banked hard to the west, but this time it wavered and shook and refused to level off. Mehlat shouted something in Turkish. A worried wrinkle crossed Uncle Mason's brow. Rachel watched the dusty ground swell closer until it filled the entire window. Something was wrong. They were going to crash!

The rear of the plane bounced off the dirt and lunged forward, throwing Rachel and the Baggy Pants twins to the floor of the cargo area. Mehlat shouted again, this time in English, his hands flipping madly at the toggle switches lining the cockpit control panel. Uncle Mason clenched both fists around the flight stick between them and yanked backward.

The last things Rachel remembered were fruit from Uncle Mason's basket bouncing through the cargo area and the terrified look in the toothless woman's eyes. Then came a thunderous crash, and everything went black.

## CHAPTER 3

"Welcome to Dogubeyazit! May your soul be safe from harm!"

Mehlat's voice echoed through the dusty innards of the plane. Rachel found herself upside down in the center of the cargo area. The only thing between her and the travel trunks was the bump on her head.

"You sound pretty cheerful for a man who just landed an airplane with only one working propeller and no landing gear," Rachel heard Uncle Mason say. "How bad is the damage?"

"Not bad. I say two days, and we fly again." Rachel detected a smile in Mehlat's voice.

Uncle Mason unbuckled and peeked around the side of his seat. His beard was bloodied where his chin had struck the flight stick.

"Elliot, Rachel. You two all right?"

"I think so," came Elliot's weary reply.

Rachel, her head still smarting, didn't bother to answer. Baggy Pants One and Baggy Pants Two had shifted the trunks aside and lifted her onto the bench seat next to Elliot. Even the toothless woman got involved, offering to tie her scarf around Rachel's banged-up skull.

"No, I'm fine, really," Rachel insisted. "Thanks anyway." She tried to return the scarf but the woman, whose eyes now spoke kindness instead of fear, refused.

"Please," she said, pressing Rachel's hands around the colored cloth. "Keep, keep."

Within minutes, a rickety bus chugged alongside the crippled airplane. A young black-haired man hopped from the driver's seat and quickly ferried their luggage from the cargo area into shallow compartments hidden on each side of the bus. Just as quickly, he returned to the bus and waited for them to board.

Uncle Mason and Mehlat talked for several minutes and examined the airplane. Rachel followed Elliot from the dented plane to the battered bus. Riding in dangerous vehicles seemed to be a Turkish custom she would have to get used to. As she stepped aboard, Rachel remembered the scarf in her hands. But when she turned to thank the toothless woman, she and the Baggy Pants Twins were gone.

"We're headed for a hotel downtown," Elliot informed Rachel. He pointed in the direction opposite the foothills and the fairy-tale palace toward an open, spreading plain. A dismal collection of patchy, flat-roofed buildings sprawled in the distance.

"That's it? That's Dog Biscuit?"

"Guess so," answered Elliot as they sat down. "It's even the same color as a dog biscuit."

Rachel shook her head and closed her eyes. "Please tell me this is all a terrible dream. Then wake me up, quick."

Before Rachel could open her eyes, Uncle Mason had bid Mehlat a fond good-bye and climbed onto the bus. He sat across the aisle from Rachel, and as the bus lurched forward, he nodded at the scarf twisting in Rachel's hands. "I see you've snagged your first artifact."

"I didn't want it. But that woman insisted I keep the thing."

"I'm sure she did. She wanted you to carry the scarf with you, probably for good luck. Kind of a Kurdish custom."

"Yeah, Rachel. A Kurdish rabbit's foot," Elliot added. Suddenly the bus swerved, narrowly missing a dip in the roadway, tossing them in their seats. "See, it's working already."

Uncle Mason shifted his big frame in his seat. "Okay, you two. We need to lay down a few ground rules now that we've arrived in Dogubeyazit," he said.

He paused a moment to collect his thoughts. Rachel already knew the basic rules for the dig site. Elliot and Uncle Mason had briefed her on tent pitching, campsite manners, protection from the sun, and on how to move around the dig without destroying some priceless piece of old junk. And Uncle Mason had told them a little about the Kurds—the Baggy Pants People—living in Dog Biscuit and on the nearby mountain slopes. She couldn't imagine what else they needed to know.

"Ground Rule One," Uncle Mason said. "Stick together.

There is a great deal of unrest in eastern Turkey, especially here in the countryside. The Kurds are good people, proud people. But they don't always agree with the Turkish government, and they don't always agree with each other. Neither group is particularly trusting of strangers. So traveling alone can be dangerous."

"But Mehlat is Turkish and he has lots of Kurdish friends," Elliot observed.

"True. But Mehlat understands their ways. He admires their spunk."

"He nearly spunked all of us in that so-called airplane of his," huffed Rachel.

"He's a Turkish military officer," said Uncle Mason. "And without the government's say-so, we can't continue our work at the digs. Mehlat is our ticket in and out of here.

"Ground Rule Two. Keep your eyes and ears open. There is much to see and learn here. Armut, a local guide and trusted friend, will meet us in town. You can learn a lot from him. I owe the success of this dig to Armut."

Rachel liked the sound of that name—Armut. It sounded like a cow . . . "Ar-mooooot."

"Ground Rule Three is simple but important. It's the Golden Rule: treat everyone you meet the same way you wish to be treated. None of us can go wrong with that one."

Fifteen minutes later the bus screeched to a halt at the door of the hotel in beautiful downtown flat-roofed, brick-and-plaster Dog Biscuit. The hotel desk clerk inside seemed nice enough, although he spoke little

English. Uncle Mason confirmed their reservations, and the clerk arranged to have their bags taken to adjoining rooms facing the street. Then he and another man wrestled both travel trunks into a storage room next to the lobby.

"Has Armut arrived?" Uncle Mason asked.

The clerk flashed a wide grin. "Yes, yes. Armut is here, at the teahouse." He pointed across the dusty street to a building that looked exactly like every other building in the city.

A teahouse in Dog Biscuit? Rachel was stunned. Tea meant civilization, something she had not expected to find for at least eight more days. Nothing sounded better to her at that moment than a nice spot of tea, just as she remembered enjoying every afternoon in Great Britain. Maybe she wasn't so tired after all. Elliot and Uncle Mason planned to nap all afternoon. She would slip over to the teahouse, relax over a cup of tea, and return before anyone noticed she was gone.

A short hallway guided them to their rooms, which were nothing to write home about; in fact, they were shabby by Rachel's standards, but they would do for one night.

Rachel plopped limply on her bed the moment they reached the rooms.

"I am exhausted," she sighed, stretching her arms above her head in a forced yawn. "You two go on. I believe I'll lie down awhile."

"We should all get a little shut-eye," said Uncle Mason, rubbing his injured chin. "There's a good restaurant down the street. Let's rest for a few hours, then have dinner and plan our strategy for tomorrow."

Rachel nodded sleepily. Slowly, she closed the door connecting her room with theirs, then pressed her ear against it. She listened for several minutes until she was certain they had fallen asleep.

Teatime! She would wash up and pop over to the teahouse, then be back in time for dinner. Washing up, however, presented a problem. There were no towels, no washcloths, no sinks. There wasn't even a bathroom. So *that's* what Uncle Mason meant when he said the hotel had *basic* accommodations. No water. It didn't matter. She could wash up with tea, if need be, at the teahouse.

She slipped her backpack over her shoulder. Quietly, she closed her room door and tiptoed down the hallway to the hotel lobby. The desk clerk greeted her again, smiling broadly.

"Your room . . . everything is fine?" he asked in broken English.

"Oh, just fine. Although I suppose a room with running water might be too much to ask," Rachel replied flippantly. "Now, I believe you said there is a teahouse nearby?"

"Yes," he nodded, again pointing through the hotel lobby window to a plaster-walled shop across the street.

"Thank you very much," Rachel said curtly. She headed for the door.

The clerk's smile faded.

"But . . . but, you should not . . . it is best . . . ," he stammered.

"I know which tea is best. I've been drinking tea all of my life. I only hope they know how to brew it." Rachel felt a certain satisfaction as the door slapped shut behind her, silencing the stammering clerk.

"Now," she said aloud to herself, "let's see about that cup of tea."

She cinched up her backpack and stepped from the hotel's brick walkway into the street. Suddenly the screeching sound of worn brakes squealed in her ears and a rush of hot air blasted her hair from around her shoulders. A horn blared from behind the grille of a rusted bus bearing down upon her. Rachel jumped back just in time to avoid becoming a Turkish pancake. The faces in the windows turned toward her as the bus passed. She threw them a rude look and crossed the dirty roadway.

The teahouse was hardly what she had expected. Squatty tables and stool chairs dotted the street's edge like square wooden islands in a sea of dust. Half a dozen old men, all sporting baggy pants and hats or stocking caps, milled around in front of the teahouse. Remembering Uncle Mason's descriptions, Rachel assumed they all were Kurdish. Near the door sat three men, two playing a friendly game of backgammon, the third staring blankly at the mountains beyond the city. Through the open door Rachel spied another handful of men, and a boy, about her age, sitting inside on low chairs. The strong smell of coffee floated out the doorway.

"Good afternoon," Rachel said in a grown-up voice. She didn't expect an answer because she hadn't addressed them in gibberish. But she felt she should say something because all of the men outside the tea-house, except the mountain watcher, stopped what they were doing to stare at her.

To her amazement, one of the backgammon players lowered his chin and spoke softly.

"Good day."

"You speak English?" asked Rachel.

He nodded.

"Perhaps I can get a good cup of tea here after all," she said. She loosened the straps of her backpack.

"You are from Europe?" said the man.

"Yes, as a matter of fact I am," Rachel said. "Great Britain. But how did you know?"

The wrinkles in his olive-skinned face deepened with his smile. "Your accent."

"Of course. Are you familiar with Great Britain? Have you traveled there?"

"We have many tourists in Dogubeyazit," he replied slowly. Rachel wondered why he didn't answer her questions. "We hear many accents." He propped one foot against an empty stool. Rachel noticed the unusual black-and-white pattern in his pants. They looked almost like a zebra, except much baggier.

"What brings you to Turkey?" he continued.

"Oh, Thanksgiving usually does that," she joked. The circle of men remained silent and serious. Rachel felt her smile pale, and she quickly cleared her throat. "No, actually I'm here for a dig."

She had begun to like the sound of the word "dig." It brought an air of importance to most conversations, especially when Uncle Mason said it. And this conversation was no exception. At the mention of a dig, a portly man inside the teahouse rose from his chair and stepped out into the afternoon heat. The boy with him followed.

Mr. Zebra Pants raised his eyebrows. His backgammon opponent grunted and adjusted the turbanlike scarf surrounding the top of his head. Then he spoke.

"Turkey is a land of digs, a land of ancient peoples. This is where all of time began."

Rachel had already stuck her foot in her mouth once with the turkey joke. She wasn't about to repeat her mistake by discussing archeology with a group of grumpy Kurdish men.

A scratchy voice shattered the awkward silence. It came from Rachel's back.

*"Var! Var!"*

Startled, she jerked around to find the mountain watcher, who had made his way from the shadows of the teahouse to stand behind her.

"You nearly scared me out of my . . ." Her voice tightened into a gasp. The old man behind her looked as though he had climbed from a nightmare. Long fingernails poked like claws from his raised hands. A dingy turban swaddled his head. And below his wild eyebrows lay two glassy eyes the color of milk. He was blind.

*"Var!"* he cried again, groping toward her.

"What is he saying?" said Rachel, backing away from the shouting man.

"Do you not see, little woman?" replied the Kurd in

the turban. "He is a foolish old man, afraid of his own shadow." Rachel deliberately placed herself on the opposite side of one of the small tables, careful to keep it between her and the nightmare.

"He keeps yelling '*Var.*' What does it mean?" she blurted.

"He is telling you that it exists," laughed the man.

"What exists?"

"The mountain. Old Tuz thinks he has discovered the great mountain." The Kurd stood and pointed to the immense mountain filling the horizon to the northeast. Then he turned to face the white-bearded blind man. "Of course it exists, Old Tuz. When we look to the east, Ararat is *all* we see!"

"Perhaps it is large enough that even *he* sees it!" chimed Mr. Zebra Pants. Both men laughed and nodded to one another.

Old Tuz ignored the men and their laughter. He spit onto the brick sidewalk bordering the teahouse and pulled at his shabby woolen vest. As he did so, Rachel noticed a curious amulet dangling around his scrawny neck. The necklace appeared to be made from a chunk of very old, darkened wood. Etched marks covered the surface of it. More gibberish, Rachel thought to herself. Chicken scratchings.

It was then that a loud voice echoed through the dusty street. It belonged to Uncle Mason, standing beside the hotel. He was frowning.

"Rachel! Rachel, come here! Now!"

Elliot stood with him in the hotel doorway, shaking his head.

A hand gently squeezed Rachel's shoulder. She found herself sandwiched between the portly man who had emerged from the teahouse and the olive-skinned boy at his side.

"We should go now," the man said quietly. "Your uncle is waiting."

"How did you know . . ."

"Please," the man insisted. "We go." Without another word he led Rachel and the boy toward the hotel. In the confusion, the frightening old man suddenly lashed out and grabbed Rachel by the straps of her backpack. She found herself staring into the clouded eyes of blind Old Tuz, close enough to count every yellow tooth and gray hair. The amulet and its chicken scratchings swung from his neck like a pendulum above her forehead. Old Tuz's weathered face grew frenzied and urgent.

"*Var,*" he whispered softly, so that only Rachel could hear. "I have seen it. It is there, on the mountain that burns within."

# CHAPTER 4

"What do you suppose that old man at the teahouse was jabbering about?" Rachel asked, clutching the saddle horn in front of her with both hands. She steadied herself against the slow, bumpy gait of her horse, just as she had done the past three hours, as they plodded toward the dig site in the stony foothills outside Dog Biscuit. Sunrise had come too soon for Rachel, and a poor night's sleep in a dusty hotel hadn't erased the frightening memory of the teahouse and the old Kurd with white eyes and yellow teeth.

Elliot answered exactly as Rachel expected he would.

"If you had followed Ground Rule One and not gone out alone, you wouldn't have crossed a jabbering old man. You're lucky Armut and Yedi showed up. If they hadn't escorted you out of there, Old Tuz might have had you for lunch."

"A jolly lot of help *they* were," Rachel huffed. "That old guy grabbed me right out from under their noses. I might have been killed."

Little did Elliot know, Rachel had broken all *three*

ground rules the very first day. She had wandered off alone, she ignored signs of danger at the teahouse, and she had snapped at the desk clerk as a frog snaps at flies. But those trivial slipups would be her own little secret.

"Old Toot, or whatever his name was, said he had seen something up in the mountains," Rachel recounted. "How could he see anything? He's blind."

"Gee, Rachel, I don't know," Elliot teased. "Maybe you should go back to the teahouse and ask him. I'm sure he'd love another visit from you."

"Oh, cork it," Rachel snapped. She searched through her mental checklist of rude responses, hoping to find just the right one for Elliot. Comparing his brain to that of a cockroach's came to mind. But before she could blurt out a reply, the horses crested a foothill and Elliot interrupted her thoughts.

"Goodness Agnes! Would you look at this place!"

They had reached the dig site. To the south stood the fairy-tale Saray Palace on the crown of a rocky foothill. Beyond it, a flat plain of wheat stubble glistened with morning dew. Behind them lay the flat roofs of sleeping Dog Biscuit. Straight ahead loomed the jagged mountains of Ararat, casting their cold blue shadows over the narrow plateau that stretched before Rachel's eyes.

Two distinct peaks towered above the others in the backbone chain of mountains. Elliot had pestered her all the way to the dig site, rattling off statistics on the twin peaks. As if Rachel were interested. She tried not to pay much attention, but she had learned from

Elliot's lecture that the two tallest peaks had names:
Lesser Ararat to the east, which was the smaller of the
two, and Greater Ararat next to it. They were connected by a saddle-shaped mass of rock and ice. But as far
as Rachel was concerned, mountains were mountains.
She had seven days (and counting) to stare at them.

The dig site was smaller than she had expected,
maybe half as big as a football field. And it looked boring. Except for the five of them—Rachel, Elliot, Uncle
Mason, Armut, and his skinny nephew, Yedi—and
their horses, the dig was empty. Nothing but dirt,
rough grass, and scrubby bushes. Weird blocks of
gray stone covered with chicken scratchings poked
from the flattened foothill. The only sounds were the
whistling of the wind and the jingling of bells that dec-
orated Yedi's saddlebags.

Uncle Mason and Armut, who were riding in the
lead, stopped abruptly. Uncle Mason turned in his saddle and glanced over his shoulder.

"We're here," he said simply. "You can see why it's
best to travel these foothills on horseback. Much more
dependable than a bus. Probably safer as well." He dismounted and began rifling through his saddlebags.
Armut did the same.

"If we're lucky, the bus will be here soon with the
travel trunks and the work tent," Uncle Mason informed
them while checking his watch. "Assuming, that is,
that the driver doesn't spend all morning shuttling
tourists from town to the Saray."

Yedi clucked to his horse with his tongue and tugged
the reins lightly. The mare turned a tight circle, carry-

ing Yedi and his jingling bells around the edge of the dig site and back to where Elliot and Rachel sat atop their horses. A light gray woolen jacket clung to his shoulders, partly covering a crude sweater beneath. His traditional baggy pants flapped in the mountain breeze against his saddle. Rachel watched him guide his horse next to hers.

"This is it?" Rachel sputtered, feeling much the same as she had when she first laid eyes on Dog Biscuit. She felt her jaw drop open in shock. "This squatty little patch of dirty pasture? We traveled thousands of miles just to sleep on the ground at this place?"

A worried look crossed Yedi's face.

"Are you feeling well?" he asked her. "Your mouth . . . it is open very wide."

Instantly Rachel clamped her jaw shut. She met Yedi with a stare meant to burn holes through him.

"Actually, I don't feel too well," she said in a mocking voice. "Would you mind terribly, taking me home to Kentucky? I hope it isn't too much trouble!" She squinted and wrinkled up her nose when she said the word "trouble," just to get her point across.

"She's not always like this, Yedi," defended Elliot. "Sometimes she really gets cranky." He climbed from his horse.

Rachel would have been happy to hop from her horse and dig through her saddlebags like everyone else. She didn't particularly like horses anyway, especially the one that had nipped her backside several years ago at a riding stable in Great Britain. But she had a small problem. Her right stirrup had twisted, wedging her foot crosswise so she couldn't move it. To make matters worse, Armut had cinched the tail of her jacket between her saddle and the fat old mare's belly when he tightened the saddle in the dark back in Dog Biscuit. She couldn't rise up, and she couldn't climb down.

"Rachel," Elliot said with a hint of sarcasm in his voice, "do you plan to get off that horse anytime soon, like, in this century?"

"I rather enjoy the view from up here," she replied quickly, covering her dilemma. "It's been years since I've ridden."

"Right. Twenty years, at least," Elliot quipped to Yedi.

"You are wise," Yedi said to Rachel. "If I could have only two things, I, too, would want only a view of the mountains and a horse to explore them."

"Finally!" Rachel sighed to Elliot. "Someone who appreciates the finer things in life—like a woman's wisdom." The whole time she was talking, she squirmed and twisted her foot. It wouldn't budge.

"So," Elliot asked again, "are you coming?"

"In a minute. You two go on."

"Suit yourself," Elliot said, adjusting the tilt of his hat. He led his horse over to join Uncle Mason and Armut's horses nipping at the short pasture nearby.

Yedi quietly slipped from his horse. He clucked his tongue and his horse dutifully followed Elliot. Then, without a word, Yedi reached up, grasped Rachel's stirrup and, with a graceful twist of his wrist, Rachel's foot popped free. Another simple tug loosened her jacket from beneath the saddle. Yedi smiled up at her in a way that made her feel stupid and small.

"We should unload our belongings now, before the bus arrives," he said quietly, still smiling.

Great. Just what Rachel needed. *Two* know-it-alls—first Elliot and now Baggy Pants Junior, whose name sounded like some sort of tropical birdcall . . . "Ya-DEE, Ya-DEE!"

She waited for Yedi to join the others, then hesitantly crawled from her horse's back, keeping both hands tightly around the saddle until her dangling feet touched the ground.

"First it was crashing airplanes, then a rickety bus, and now I have to travel on a stubborn animal like you," Rachel muttered. "Well? Go on you stupid horse. Go eat with your friends." She pointed toward the cluster of horses' tails nearby, but the old mare just stared at her with big droopy eyes. "All right, suit yourself. But don't come running to me when you're hungry and there's no grass left. You're as stubborn as Elliot," she added, pointing a finger in the poor horse's face. For a moment, she imagined Elliot's face looking back at her, saying: *Remember Ground Rule Three.*

Rachel noticed the sun had risen above Lesser Ararat. The smaller peak now cast its conelike shadow in a sharp outline along the massive side of Greater Ararat, pointing like an arrow toward its higher summit. Already, clouds had begun to gather near the taller mountain's tip. She slipped off her jacket as the warm sunshine stretched over the mountains, quickly chasing away the morning's chill.

Baggy Pants Junior was following Uncle Mason

around like a puppy dog. His hands clutched a rough-looking piece of reddish-brown mud shaped into a flat brick the size of a book.

"*Effendi* Mason," Yedi said, "I have something for you. From the mountain." He passed the brick from his skinny fingers into Uncle Mason's big hands.

"Well, well, what have we here?" Uncle Mason asked politely.

"A clay tablet. I found it on the north side of the mountain. At the monastery. I believe it is very old."

Uncle Mason held the tablet at arm's length and studied it through squinted eyes. The writing on the clay was little more than small scratches and tick marks carved into its surface. Rachel wasn't surprised when Uncle Mason slipped his spectacles from his pocket and pinched them onto the tip of his nose.

"This is a magnificent specimen," he said. "Perfect condition."

Yedi smiled.

"Definitely Sumerian origin," continued Uncle Mason's appraisal. "From the looks of it, the cuneiform script is Akkadian style. Common stuff, really. Usually not too exciting. The Akkadians wrote down everything—laws, business deals, bills, family stories, even jokes. I'm surprised they didn't make greeting cards. I'll have to take a closer look, of course, to be certain, but this tablet must be at least 3,000 years old. Where did you say you got it? At the old monastery?"

"Yes," said Yedi. "Inside the box."

"Box, eh?" Uncle Mason mumbled, half to himself, still studying the tablet intently. He ran his fingers slowly across the tablet's face, feeling each dented arrow and sharp line carved into the clay. The tablet looked as hard as stone, but Uncle Mason handled it gingerly, as if it were as brittle as a cracker.

"I recognize a few of these symbols. This one stands for 'donkey.' And this one down here," he said, pointing to a chicken scratching in the center of the tablet, "means 'grain' or 'hay.'" He smiled. "Probably a Sumerian woman's shopping list for the barn."

Finally he lifted the pinchy glasses from his nose and looked at Yedi. His right eyebrow raised a question.

"You say this was inside a box? What sort of box?"

"A shiny box. Like a mirror in the sun. I will show you." Yedi walked to his horse and fished around inside his dusty saddlebags. Moments later, a burnished chest appeared in his hands, glistening in the sunlight. It was barely bigger than the clay tablet, and the corners were rounded smooth. Fine scrolling designs framed the edges. Three rosy jewels sparkled on the lid.

"Goodness Agnes!" Uncle Mason exclaimed.

"Now that's what I call a box!" said Elliot.

It was lovely. A bit too flashy for Rachel's tastes; still, she thought, it might look nice on her dresser back home.

Uncle Mason carefully set the clay tablet on a nearby boulder and lifted the box from Yedi's hands. He turned it slowly. The jewels on the lid shone like tiny rainbows.

"Are there any other boxes like this, Yedi?" asked Uncle Mason.

"I do not think so," Yedi replied.

"No, I doubt that there are," echoed Uncle Mason, his eyes glancing from the box to the tablet and back to the box again. "This chest seems to have been created for only one purpose—to protect this clay tablet."

"I will be happy to go and look for more boxes, *Effendi* Mason," offered Yedi.

"I think not," Armut quietly interrupted. He smiled at Uncle Mason. "Yedi should not have gone to the monastery the first time. Like many places on the mountain, it is not safe. But what is an uncle to do with such a roaming, curious boy?"

So. Yedi was a snoop. Rachel liked that. Maybe he wasn't so bad after all.

Uncle Mason opened the lid of the shiny container. Inside, the chest was lined with folds of heavy silk—deep purple—flecked with tiny pieces of reddish-brown dust from the clay artifact. Back home, Rachel would have viewed this "treasure" as a cheap jewelry chest stuffed with mud-splattered curtains from some garage sale. But to everyone else, standing in the shadow of the great mountain, surrounded by ancient blocks of carved stone tablets poking from the ground, the chest became mysterious.

"This chest isn't nearly as old as the tablet," observed Uncle Mason. "See the scroll work along the corners here? Probably European. Looks like something from the 1800s, but I wouldn't bet my safari hat on it."

Rachel felt like a bored college student in one of Uncle Mason's classrooms as he pointed out quirky little things on the box to the others. Old dates, clay slabs covered with chicken scratchings, scroll work . . . no wonder she slept through sixth-grade history class. Scary as he was, Rachel found Old Toot from the teahouse much more interesting.

"Mind if I keep these two artifacts for a while?" Uncle Mason finally asked Armut. "I'd like to decipher the cuneiform writing and see what it says. That Sumerian woman must have written up one whale of a shopping list if the monks at the monastery made a special chest like this to keep it in."

Armut nodded toward Yedi. "The boy found them. They are his treasures and, therefore, they are his responsibility."

"I would be pleased for you to have them, *Effendi* Mason," Yedi said. "I am very anxious to know what the words mean." Then he slyly added, "Maybe the Sumerian woman had a very big barn."

Rachel found herself laughing along with everyone else. Yedi was more than just a snoop. He was a polite, funny snoop. She liked that even better.

# CHAPTER 5

The bus from Dog Biscuit finally made it to the dig
site, but not before the day had turned into a real
scorcher. Rachel was surprised at how quickly the cool
morning burned away in the dry mountain heat. She
had shed all but her T-shirt and shorts and, if she
believed everything Elliot told her (which she didn't),
she was asking for a nasty sunburn.

The bus driver dropped off the travel trunks and an
assortment of poles and canvas tarps for constructing a
makeshift work tent. He also dropped off sleeping cots,
nonperishable food, bottled water, and a pair of Kurdish
workers who appeared to know Armut.

True to his word, Uncle Mason set everyone straight
to work making camp. The Kurds jibbered and jab-
bered with Armut, following his every command. By
lunchtime, a green and tan canvas tent the size of a
two-car garage flapped in the constant breeze. Uncle
Mason announced that the tent would serve as a prep
area for any artifacts they uncovered, as well as provide a place to sleep.

Once the tent was up, Rachel convinced Elliot and Yedi to pack the skimpy peanut butter sandwiches from the supply bus and climb a small foothill rising from the dig site. She was anxious to get Yedi away from his uncle and learn more about his favorite places to go snooping.

"So," Rachel began, when the trio stopped to eat partway up the hill, "tell me about the old monkey house." If Yedi was such a good snoop, Rachel figured, he could surely provide her with some juicy bits of information that might make this whole expedition worthwhile. For starters, he could tell her where the old monkeys lived.

Yedi looked at her as if he wanted to answer but couldn't.

"I do not understand," he said after a long silence.

"The monkey house," pressed Rachel. "The place where you found the jeweled box and that chunk of ancient play dough."

"I think she means the monastery," said Elliot. He worked a small rock free from the dark soil and tossed it down the hillside toward the dig. Uncle Mason, Armut, and the two Kurdish helpers huddled below, already hard at work taking measurements from one of the stone pillars rising above the cleared dig site.

"Right," confirmed Rachel. "Where the monkeys live."

"Not *monkeys*, Rachel," Elliot sighed. "Monks. You know, monks? The religious guys in the brown robes with the bald heads who live in old buildings out in the middle of nowhere?"

Rachel felt her face turn fire-engine red with embarrassment. The silly smirk returned to Yedi's face. Realizing how stupid she sounded, she quickly snapped back.

"Everyone knows what a monk is," she replied, covering her goof. "It's just that, well . . . in Great Britain we used to call monkeys 'monks.'"

Elliot crossed his arms and adjusted his glasses, a sure sign that he didn't believe her.

"You know, I think you're right," Elliot agreed, surprising her. "There are two places where monkeys are called monks—in Great Britain, and on *Jupiter*." Yedi almost laughed but Rachel stifled him with a well-placed glare. Then she turned a stone face to Elliot.

"Well, Mr. Walking Dictionary, I hope you're as good at reading ancient languages on clay tablets as you are at speaking Jupiter-ese. I heard Uncle Mason say that he expects you to decode Yedi's old brick. In this lifetime."

"As Dad said, the tablet's in good shape. The symbols are easy to read."

"Easy for a Samuri woman, maybe, but not for an Indiana four-eyes like you," challenged Rachel.

"Sumerian woman," corrected Elliot. "You know," he added, smashing his half-eaten sandwich into his belt pack, "I should go back to the dig and take a closer look at that tablet."

"You don't really think you can make any sense of those scratchy marks, do you?"

"Maybe," Elliot replied. "Dad has a pretty big collection of books on ancient languages. Plus I've read some stuff about cuneiform writing."

Elliot seemed like such a genius sometimes. Rachel wished that, just once, she could know something he didn't.

"Humph," she grumped. "Is there anything you haven't read?"

"Mmmmm . . . let me think," Elliot pondered, resting his chin in his hand and rolling his eyes. "There was . . . no, I've read that. How about . . . no, I've read that, too."

"Oh, stop it!" Rachel hollered.

"The dictionary," teased Elliot. "I haven't read the dictionary yet. I'm only up to the letter *P*."

"Oh good. So you've read what it means to be a pea-brain."

"Well . . . I've read that some dinosaurs had brains the size of a pea."

"Especially the *Ellio-saurus rex*," Rachel said sarcastically.

"Ho-ho-ho," Elliot responded, with what sounded like a poor imitation of a sickly Santa Claus. "We'll see who's laughing when I crack the code on that tablet. Maybe it's a treasure map to a lost gold mine."

"*I* hope it is something dreadful, like instructions for changing 3,000-year-old baby diapers!"

"I hope not," Elliot gasped, hiding a smile. "I've already read about that." He winked at Yedi, which steamed Rachel even more. Then he turned and clambered down the hillside to the dig.

"Oh, go on then!" Rachel called after him. "Go stare at your stupid clay brick. Yedi and I have more important things to do."

Yedi, who hadn't said a word during all of the bickering, looked bewildered.

"What important thing do we have to do?" he wondered.

"I don't know. There must be something." She thought for a moment. This seemed like the perfect time to combine Yedi's power of snoopery with her own.

"I say we go to the monkey . . . I mean, monastery. And look for boxes," she schemed.

Yedi shook his head. "No, it is too far."

"How far?" asked Rachel.

"A full day's travel. To the distant side of the mountain," said Yedi, pointing over Mount Ararat.

"Ohhh." Rachel groaned, playing up her disappointment.

"Besides, *Apo* is right," he went on. "The old monastery is a dangerous place to go."

"*Apo*? Who is *Apo*?"

"Uncle Armut. *Apo* is Kurdish for 'Uncle.'"

Rachel felt a smile squirm onto her face. "I rather like that name. Ar-mooooot. Reminds me of the sad-eyed cows back in Kentucky."

Yedi laughed in a high-pitched giggle that made Rachel laugh with him.

"What's so funny?" she asked.

"Apo," Yedi said, still giggling. "Sounding like a sad-eyed cow!" Yedi sounded so goofy that Rachel just had to laugh again. Finally, through the giggles, he said, "And Armut is not his real name."

"Really? Then why do you call him Armut?"

"All of the Turks in Dogubeyazit call him Armut. It is Turkish for 'pear.'"

"Pear?"

"Yes. They call him Armut because his body is shaped like a big pear." Yedi drew the shape of a pear fruit in the air with his hands and out slipped another high-pitched giggle.

As their giggles died away, Rachel asked him, "So, how long until your summer visit with Armut is over?"

"What do you mean?" he said, sounding puzzled.

"When will you go home?"

"This is my home."

"You live with Armut?" Rachel felt her jaw to make sure it wasn't hanging open this time.

"Yes. Do you not live with *Effendi* Mason?" Yedi asked.

"Are you kidding? Me, live in the same house as Elliot? Spending a week out here with him is bad enough!" Rachel flipped her hair from her shoulders. "No," she finally said. "I live with Mother. Which isn't much better than living with Elliot."

Yedi quietly lowered his eyes. Suddenly Rachel became aware of something.

"You don't have a mother, do you?" she said, searching his face. He shook his head. "Well, neither does Elliot," she informed him. Silence. Rachel felt the awkward hush between them and it made her uncomfortable. Finally she spoke.

"I'm sorry," she said. She really was sorry—sorry that Yedi had no mother, sorry she had been so blunt about it, and sorry for making her own mother sound terrible. Which she wasn't, of course. As Elliot said, her mother tended to forget things—things like Rachel. But she wasn't all that bad.

"Well," Rachel added, hoping to lighten things up a bit, "I guess living with Uncle Mason might not be so bad after all. Maybe I could keep Elliot in a cage or something."

Yedi smiled slowly. "I suppose Apo is my mother." He let out a small giggle. "And, as long as you are here, *Effendi* Mason is *your* mother."

"Why do you call Uncle Mason *effendi*?" Rachel wondered.

"He is in charge of the dig. *Effendi* shows respect for his age and wisdom." Yedi paused, then stifled a giggle. "I call him *effendi* because he is a wise guy."

"A wise guy?" The smile on Yedi's face told Rachel he was making a joke. "Oh, you're a sneaky one, aren't you?" she chided him.

Yedi stood up. "We should return to the dig now," he said.

"Wait, wait!" Rachel begged, still hoping to draw out his snoopiness. "You haven't told me about the monastery. What does it look like?"

"Oh, it does not look like anything," he said as he started down the low hillside. "It is no longer there."

"It didn't just grow legs and walk away, did it?" she goaded him, following his steps down the hill. "After all, where can a whole monastery full of monks go?"

Yedi didn't stop until they reached the work tent, which by now was cluttered with equipment and supplies. Then he turned to answer her.

"The mountain swallowed it."

"That's ridiculous!" Rachel said. "Now you're starting to sound just like Elliot."

An instant later, Elliot's head poked from behind a side flap of the work tent.

"What's ridiculous?" he asked.

"You are," Rachel jumped in before Yedi could answer. "Go back to gawking at that musty tablet. This private conversation is none of your business."

"I told her the monastery was swallowed by the mountain," said Yedi.

"In a manner of speaking, it was," Elliot said calmly.

"See?" Rachel turned on Yedi. "You've dragged him into it. Now we'll have to survive Mr. Encyclopedia's lecture on the digestive systems of mountains."

"This area is famous for its earthquakes," Elliot began, just as Rachel feared he would. "Back in 1840 a real peak popper rolled across the northern slopes of Mount Ararat. Turned the monastery into one gigantic waffle and buried it under a syrup of black lava from inside the mountain. It's all part of a glacier now. I don't know how you found your way up to the old site, Yedi."

"There is more than one way to skin a goat," Yedi said proudly.

"Yuk," Rachel huffed. She didn't like goats any better than she liked horses. But the thought of skinning one made her ill.

Their first afternoon on the dig whizzed by. Rachel helped organize equipment and set up a worktable under the tent canopy. Uncle Mason even showed her how to use some of the tools tucked deep into the travel trunk. By evening, Yedi and Elliot had kindled a small campfire from wood delivered on the Dog Biscuit bus. The closest tree around stood nearly a mile away.

Armut roasted a big hunk of mystery meat over the fire for their supper, but it didn't smell quite right to Rachel. After all that talk about skinning goats, she had lost her appetite. She skipped the meat, ate half a box of graham crackers instead, and drank two bottles of water.

After supper, everyone huddled around the meager campfire while Uncle Mason fetched a lantern. The faces surrounding Rachel glowed orange in the firelight. Only a few hours ago, in the blazing August heat, she couldn't bear the thought of a campfire. But now, in the chill of evening, there was no place she would rather be.

"Tell us a story, Apo," Yedi asked, pulling his blue turban tighter over his ears. "Tell us a story from the mountain."

"Ah, the mountain," said Armut in a hushed voice. With a grunt, he crossed his legs Indian-style, which was no small feat for a man of Armut's size and shape. He lowered his head for a moment as if to concentrate his thoughts. Then he looked up at them and his eyes shone as brightly as the fire itself. His thick hand emerged from beneath his woolen cloak and pointed toward the twin peaks of Ararat, fading in the purple light of sunset.

"The mountain is home to many mysteries," he began. "There are those who have lived to tell of the mysteries, and there are those who have climbed its slopes and never returned."

"I think we should send Elliot up the mountain," Rachel interjected, "just to see if he ever returns."

Armut cleared his throat. "The story is told of a man who sent his donkey out from the village of Eli, along the mountainside, to find fresh pasture. It was a summer evening much like this one, with the dim fires of shepherd camps flickering in the coming darkness. At dusk the man heard his donkey's brays echoing down to the village. He listened from the safety of his shelter as night crept onto the mountain, until suddenly the donkey grew quiet. The man waited and listened. The night remained silent. But his donkey did not return."

Yedi grinned from ear to ear. Obviously he had heard this story before.

"The man called to the donkey in the darkness, again and again," continued Armut, his eyes jumping like flames from face to face. "And still there came no answer. Finally he wrapped himself in a woolen blanket, lit a torch from his campfire, and slowly edged his way along the rocky mountainside. The familiar sounds of the sheep and their dogs were absent. Even the wind seemed to speak in whispers. When he reached the place where the donkey had been feeding, he heard a muffled sound curling around his feet. He lowered his torch to the earth and . . ."

"Wait, wait!" Rachel interrupted again. "I've heard this one. He lowered his torch and he saw a teeny tiny woman with a teeny tiny nose, carrying a bone. And then this scary voice behind her says, 'Give me my bone' and the teeny tiny woman says . . . , 'TAKE IT!'" Rachel yelled "Take it!" so loudly that everyone sitting around the campfire jumped.

Uncle Mason bolted from the tent, his lantern swinging wildly in his fist.

"Goodness Agnes!" he shouted. "What in the world . . ."

As the echo of Uncle Mason's voice hung in the night air, Armut raised his arm for silence and spoke again.

"Oh no, dear one," he said to Rachel, keeping a serious face. "There was no teeny tiny woman. The torchlight revealed two glassy yellow eyes, as large as fists, glistening at the man's feet. They were the eyes of a snake—an enormous snake with a bump in its belly the size of a donkey."

"Yuk," Rachel said, quietly announcing her disgust.

"And then what happened?" Elliot had to ask.

"We shall never know," Armut responded. "For that man is one who never returned from the mountain." Then his face slowly cracked a smile.

"Telling the old donkey-snake story again, are we, Armut?" chuckled Uncle Mason as he took his place among them by the fire.

"Yes, Effendi Mason," Yedi jumped in. "Apo is telling us stories of the mountain."

Uncle Mason poked at the fire's embers and shook his head. "Oh, Armut's got a million of 'em," he laughed again. "Has he told the one about the two wild dogs, the shepherd, and the lightning bolt?"

Armut laughed heartily. "Maybe tomorrow night."
He looked again toward Ararat, which by now had
become a giant shadow below the stars. A thoughtful
expression swept over his face.

"There is one true mystery," he told them. "A mystery as old as time itself." Armut uncrossed his legs
with another grunt and slowly rose to his feet. His
shadow followed him, looking like a giant black pear
with legs, sneaking up behind him. As Armut moved
closer to the dying fire, Rachel scooted closer too.

"You see, my people come from the mountain. The
mountain is part of us, and we are part of it. We belong
to one another. And the mystery is this: how can a people, who are flesh and bone, arise from a mountain of
stone and ice? How can jagged rock be our mother, or
frozen snow our father? The answer lies in a time
before our own—in a time long ago before clay tablets
and stone pillars."

Armut was talking nonsense now, as far as Rachel
was concerned. She had hoped the true mystery
involved a ghost, or a giant hairy man, or something
really terrifying, not some babbling about rocks and
mothers.

"At one time, men and animals moved freely among
each other," Armut went on. "They walked side by side
and shared the land. And before that time passed, my
people found themselves on the great mountain.
Together with the animals they came down to settle in
the foothills where their sheep and goats grew fat. In
summer, the mountain gave them green meadows and
cool water. In winter's harsh cold, they warmed them-

selves on the beating heart of the mountain itself."

Snakes on the mountain? Sure, Rachel could go for that. Giant hairy men? Maybe. But not beating hearts. No way. Besides, what was scary about beating hearts?

"The mountain has many names," Armut said at last. "The Turks call it Agri-Dagi. To others it is the Mountain of Nu-Wah, or Mount Ararat. But for my people it is The Cradle. It is the cradle that rocked us at our birth."

"There's nothing mysterious about that story," Rachel said. "You just made it up, like all of the other stories."

Armut looked at her squarely. "There is an old saying," he cautioned. "It is this: 'You need not believe something for it to be true.'"

# CHAPTER 6

"I'm dying here, you know," Rachel whined aloud, doing her best to feel sorry for herself. "We've been here three days and I'm dying of boredom. And of sunburn," she added with a groan. Gingerly, she dragged a finger across her tender pink nose. "Ouch! And nobody cares. You don't care, do you?"

Only one of the half-dozen horses chomping breakfast from the dry pasture beside the dig site bothered to look up. After letting out a couple of loud snorts, the mare bent her head to the ground in search of a wildflower for dessert.

"See? You wouldn't care if I dropped dead on this spot and the vultures came and carried me off, piece by piece, would you? Would you?" The mare nodded her head toward where Rachel sat. She could have sworn the chunky old horse was smiling.

Rachel pushed herself to her feet and stomped up and down to warm her legs. A shiver ran across the back of her neck. She glanced at Yedi, who was clearing away the remains of their campfire breakfast near the work tent. For a moment Rachel almost felt guilty for not helping him. But that feeling quickly passed. Soon, she thought, the morning sun would clear Mount Ararat and the heat would again creep down the mountain, just as it did every day. She rubbed her sunburned nose once more, wincing at the pain.

The old mare let out a final snort.

"What am I doing here? I'll tell you what I'm doing here," Rachel snorted back, shaking a finger at the circle of horses. "I'm counting icicles on my nose every morning, then roasting like a Thanksgiving turkey every afternoon." She wrapped her arms inside the small blanket hugging her shoulders and shuddered. "Hot days, cold nights. It's a wonder I'm not ill. Dog Biscuit was heaven compared to this place. At least Dog Biscuit had roofs . . . and restrooms—if you could *find* them, that is!"

She walked in a slow circle, placing one foot directly in front of the other, like baby steps in a game of "Mother, May I."

"'Entertain yourself,' Elliot tells me," she muttered, blowing into her hands to warm them. "How? By dusting off dirty pieces of pottery or dipping tiny bits of clay into Uncle Mason's cleaning jars? I don't think so." She stopped pacing. "Yedi acts as if this whole expedition couldn't survive without him—getting tools for Uncle Mason, watering you dumb horses, helping cook for the Kurdish workers. And Elliot keeps his green marble eyeballs glued to that ridiculous clay brick. How am I supposed to entertain myself when there's nothing to do?"

She glanced again toward the campfire. Usually, Elliot helped Yedi clean up after their meals. But this morning Yedi was alone. Rachel hadn't seen Elliot at breakfast that morning. Come to think of it, he had missed dinner last night, too.

Tugging the blanket over her hair like a shawl, Rachel shuffled toward the work tent. A soft glow reflected from within its canvas walls. Pulling back the side flap, Rachel found Elliot hunched over the rickety worktable, squinting at some papers in the dim yellow lamplight. He held a small magnifying glass in one hand.

"Excuse me," she said rather rudely, "but did you realize that it's light outside and breakfast was over an hour ago?"

"I know," Elliot said, motionless.

"Why didn't you eat breakfast with the rest of us?" Rachel confronted him.

"I've been up all night decoding this tablet. Wait till you hear this!"

She scowled at him. "This better be good," she said with an extra cranky voice.

"Everything's all starting to make sense now!" exclaimed Elliot. "Don't you see?"

Rachel deepened her scowl. "All I see is a smelly kerosene lamp, a piece of clay with chicken scratchings all over it, and a boring boy who has spent three days under a flapping tent. And I see four more days of you holed up in here like a hermit. And then there is Yedi." Rachel huffed out a blast of frosty breath like a dragon. "I thought he was a fun snoop who would lead us on some of those adventures you promised. Turns out he won't go anywhere unless Armut the Fruit Body says it's okay!"

"No, listen! Listen!" Elliot's voice had shifted gears. For the first time since they had arrived at the dig he sounded as though a sense of adventure had finally crept into his cockroach brain. "This clay isn't just a shopping list. We knew that the moment Yedi flashed around that box from the monastery, where he found the tablet. It had to be something extraordinary. And now we know what!"

"Maybe *you* know. I still haven't the foggiest idea what you're blabbering about. You're worse than Old Toot."

"Old Tuz," corrected Elliot. "Look. Everything is here, all written down. The mountain, the flood, the ship and cargo, the shadow that points the way—it's all here!" His momentary burst of excitement slowly came under his usual control of reason and calm. Elliot backed away from the worktable and adjusted his wire-rims. Then he drew a deep breath and gave Rachel a relaxed smile below the tired sparkle in his eyes. The old, dependable Elliot had returned. For now, at least.

"I'll show you." Elliot flipped open one of Uncle Mason's old books. Inside were pages and pages of scratchy cuneiform marks, exactly like the ones on the tablet.

"This book is my Rosetta stone," he said, as if that explained everything.

Rachel threw him one of her blank stares. It seemed the wise thing to do, considering he had her completely baffled. Better to remain silent rather than say something stupid and make Elliot feel smarter than he already was.

"The Rosetta stone was a chunk of volcanic rock found nearly 200 years ago," he told her. "The pictures and symbols carved into it helped early archeologists decode ancient Egyptian writings."

"I knew that," Rachel lied.

"I told you Dad had books on ancient languages, right? This book works like a dictionary, like the Rosetta stone," he explained. "You find the symbol and the book gives you the meaning. See, here's one of the symbols Dad recognized. It means 'grain.'"

All Rachel saw were three tiny *Y*s hanging from the bottom of a tilted line.

"And this one over here means 'donkey,'" Elliot went on.

More *Y*s. More lines. Rachel felt herself getting really steamed.

"Then there is my personal favorite, the—"

"Just read the stupid thing!" Rachel finally burst out.

"I will," Elliot said patiently. "First let me explain how the symbols run together . . ."

"Oh, all right then!" Rachel interrupted again. She snatched Elliot's notes out of his hands. "I'll read it myself. I don't need to hear the whole history of the world first!" Elliot sure could be aggravating sometimes.

She squinted at his scribbled notes. "Your handwriting is harder to read than any old code." She brushed eraser dust from the sheets of paper, spread them across the worktable and began reading aloud.

*The god of the mountain spoke to the man:*
*"When the sky fills with angry clouds, call the*
*animals to yourself. Take . . . (?)"*

"What are all these question marks about?" Rachel
wondered, pointing out scribbles on Elliot's decipher-
ing paper.

"Like I tried to explain—sometimes the symbols run
together. And not all of the words are in the book. A little guesswork helped fill in a few blank spots."

Rachel read on:

*"Bring together the sheep and the goat (or*
*deer?) and the donkey.*
*Open the door of the great ship and show them*
*(their home?).*
*Take with you grain for the animals and flour*
*for yourselves. Take with you enough (some?) for*
*two seasons(?).*
*For the ground will cover(?) with water and the*
*sun hide(?) in darkness.*
*The flood will cover(?) everything your eyes see.*
*It will wash the earth clean."*

"You made this up, didn't you, Elliot Conner?"

Elliot shook his head. "Nope. That's what it says,
best that I can tell." He slipped the paper from between
Rachel's fingers and kept reading:

*After the god of the mountain spoke, rain fell to the earth. The rain fell many days.*

*The waters carried the great ship and the man(?) family(?) to the fortress of stone, to the cliffs of ice (water?). There the mountain rocked them as a mother rocks her baby.*

*After many days the rain stopped. The sun again opened(?) its face. A warm wind blew across the waters and the earth returned.*

*Now the great ship sleeps on the mountain;*
*The mountain of our birth, the mountain of our father.*
*His feet are lovely. His feet carried life to the plains.*
*And the wild ox and donkey followed him.*
*He told the birds where to fly and the sheep where to pasture. They followed his voice (song?) to the rivers.*

"This is weird," Rachel thought out loud, peering over Elliot's shoulder. "What else does it say?"

"This last part is what's really important," Elliot said in a near whisper. "It says:

*In the clouds, the great ship rests by day.*
*At night it sleeps near the highest stars, forever joined to the mountain.*
*The great ship rests in the shadow of the younger(?) mountain . . . at sunrise—when the sun rises in the warm season and before rains*

*come to the mountains.*

*The shadow of the younger mountain points the way, like the tip of a giant's arrow.*

*Like the arrow of a giant shot from his bow, it leads to the (door?) in the oldest mountain where the great ship rests.*

*The shadow points the way.*

A sigh slipped from Elliot's lips. He had to be tired, having stayed up all night long decoding the clay message.

"This tablet," he said, pausing to yawn, "is not a grocery list. It's a map. The monks knew that. And now we know that."

"A map? A map of what?"

"Not a map *of* something. A map *to* something."

"I don't get it," Rachel admitted. She pulled the blanket tighter around her shoulders.

Elliot pulled a clean sheet of paper from the worktable drawer. He drew an upside-down *V* and below it he printed "G.A." Beside it he drew a second upside-down *V*, slightly shorter than the first, and labeled it "L.A." Two Indian teepees in a snowstorm, Rachel thought.

"These are mountains. This one is Greater Ararat," he explained, tapping his pencil on the "G.A." beneath the taller teepee.

Rachel quickly caught on. Elliot was attempting to draw a diagram of some sort. "Oh, now I see. This "L.A." doohickey is supposed to be Lesser Ararat."

Elliot nodded. "The summer sun comes up here in

the east, behind Lesser Ararat." He made a circle to the right of the shorter teepee. "As the sun rises over the smaller mountain, it casts a shadow on the side of Greater Ararat. A huge shadow." He drew a dotted line from the circle across the tip of small teepee number two to a spot on teepee number one. "And the shadow's pointed tip . . ."

Rachel was way ahead of him now. ". . . Is like the arrow from a giant's bow, as the tablet says," she finished. "I can read, you know."

Elliot placed a small $X$ on the spot where the dotted line struck Greater Ararat. Then he spoke slowly and deliberately. "The shadow . . . points the way. $X$ marks the spot, Rachel."

"What do you expect to find under the $X$? Is that where your gold-plated, 3,000-year-old baby diapers are?"

Elliot smiled a tired but satisfied smile. Then he answered.

"You ever heard of Noah's ark?"

# CHAPTER 7

"Everyone's heard of Noah's ark. I'm surprised Armut hasn't told that worn-out old story around the campfire," Rachel answered. "He could even throw in a pair of snakes."

"I'm surprised too," agreed Elliot. Instantly, Rachel perked up. Any time she and Elliot agreed on something, trouble was certain to follow. And a small dose of trouble might be just the ticket to liven things up a bit.

Elliot went on. "All of the written accounts of the great Flood and the ark refer to this area here in Turkey, and to these mountains. The Bible, the Gilgamesh Epic . . ." He gestured to the clay tablet lying on the table. "Even our Sumerian woman with the barnyard," he quipped.

He reached into the travel trunk. But instead of dragging out some dreary old archeology book, he retrieved Uncle Mason's Bible.

"Why would Uncle Mason bring that? I thought you said he packs only what he really needs for an expedition."

"Dad always packs a Bible," Elliot answered. "He says that's what got him interested in archeology in the first place."

"Oh." Rachel pretended to heave a sigh of relief. "I was afraid you might be preparing to hold church services with the mountain goats or something."

"Actually," Elliot replied, "I wanted to review the story of Noah." He thumbed through the first few dog-eared pages.

"The story goes like this, Brainiac," Rachel patronized. "Noah builds an ark, the earth floods like crazy. But Noah and his boat full of smelly animals just sail away. And that's why we have so many pet stores called Noah's ark today. Simple enough for you?"

"Let's see," Elliot muttered, clearly paying her little mind. "The ark story is here in Genesis. The earth had gotten to be a pretty nasty place, peoplewise. So here's what God told Noah. . . ."

He cleared his throat and read to Rachel as if reading her a letter or a storybook.

*"So make yourself an ark of cypress wood;*

"Some Bibles call this 'gopher wood,'" Elliot added.

*"Make rooms in it and coat it with pitch inside and out. This is how you are to build it: The ark is to be 450 feet long, 75 feet wide and 45 feet high. Make a roof for it and finish the ark to within 18 inches of the top. Put a door in the side of the ark and make lower, middle and upper decks."*

Rachel listened, halfheartedly at first. This seemed like one more opportunity for Elliot to tell her something he knew that she didn't. He couldn't just read the story, of course. He had to explain words like "gopher wood." As he read, however, she listened more intently. Pictures appeared in her mind as the tale unfolded. He read on until he came to the middle of the page.

> *"You are to bring into the ark two of all living creatures, male and female, to keep them alive with you. Two of every kind of bird, of every kind of animal and of every kind of creature that moves along the ground will come to you to be kept alive. You are to take every kind of food that is to be eaten and store it away as food for you and for them."*

He continued, reading how seven pairs of clean animals and two pairs of unclean animals, whatever those were, should also be loaded up. Rachel thought all animals were unclean. Except for cats, maybe, since they always bathe themselves. Then:

> *"Seven days from now I will send rain on the earth for forty days and forty nights, and I will wipe from the face of the earth every living creature I have made."*

"Seems a bit drastic, doesn't it?" Rachel observed.

Again he read aloud, looking for details about the ark journey. Then he held up a finger.

*For forty days the flood kept coming on the
earth, and as the waters increased they lifted the
ark high above the earth. The waters rose and
increased greatly on the earth, and the ark floated
on the surface of the water.*

Here is this old man, Rachel thought, hammering
away at a huge boat made from gopher wood and seal-
ing it up with dark oily gunk so it won't sink. Then he
waits. Sure enough, the rains come. And it rains non-
stop for forty days until the ground finally cracks open
like a watermelon and water comes gushing out. No
big deal for Noah and his family, though. They just
ride along in their floating zoo, for a zillion smelly
months. *And I thought the trip from Indiana to Dog
Biscuit was bad,* she said to herself.

*Everything on dry land that had the breath of
life in its nostrils died.*

"Wait a minute," Rachel perked up. "What was that
again?"
"Everything died, Rachel. Everything and everybody.
Except Noah and his family."

*The waters flooded the earth for a hundred and
fifty days. But God remembered Noah and all the
wild animals and the livestock that were with
him in the ark, and he sent a wind over the earth
and the waters receded.*
*At the end of the hundred and fifty days the water*

*had gone down, and on the seventeenth day of the
seventh month the ark came to rest on the mountains of Ararat.*

Elliot read how Noah sent out birds to search for dry
land. Finally he ended the story.

*So Noah came out, together with his sons and
his wife and his sons' wives. All the animals and
all the creatures that move along the ground and
all the birds—everything that moves on the
earth—came out of the ark, one kind after another. Then Noah built an altar to the Lord and, taking some of all the clean animals and clean birds,
he sacrificed burnt offerings on it.*

Rachel turned up her nose. "Yuk."

She had never heard the whole story—just bits and
pieces. Maybe that was because she visited church
about as often as she visited archeology museums. But
one thing was crystal clear. This was the same story
told on the clay tablet. No doubt about it.

When he finished reading, Elliot closed the Bible and
practically beamed at her.

"All the pieces of the puzzle fit together, even the
ones from Armut," he explained.

"What's Armut got to do with a story about the earth
flooding a zillion years ago?"

Elliot tapped his head with his pointing finger.
"Ground Rule Two, remember?"

Rachel didn't remember, exactly. In fact, she didn't

remember at all. She did recall that she had broken the rule at least once, however.

"You think I'm stupid? Of course I remember. Don't you?" she challenged.

"'Keep your eyes and ears open, for there is much to see and much to learn.'"

"Well, I'm glad you can remember *something*," Rachel snooted.

"I don't know why I didn't see this sooner," Elliot rambled on. "You know that story Armut told us around the campfire?"

"Which one? He's told us stories every night, most of them disgusting—crazed wolves, spirits, spooky voices . . . and the snakes. Giant snakes. Yuk." She tried to make her "yuk" sound convincing. Deep inside, however, Rachel secretly looked forward to campfire time. It had become her only source of entertainment, especially since Yedi wouldn't take her exploring.

"The 'true mystery,' he called it," recalled Elliot. "The story about Armut's people."

Rachel gave her eyes a dramatic roll. "I remember. Rocking cradles and beating hearts. Boring stuff."

"He said his people came from the mountain, right? And they brought animals with them. Well, listen to this part again." Elliot searched the face of the tablet for a moment, then found his place among the sheets of paper where he had decoded the poemlike words:

*His feet are lovely. His feet carried life to the plains.*

"I've never known anybody with lovely feet," Rachel said. "Feet are smelly. Grandma Ashton had bunions on her feet. They poked out to one side of her little toes like big warts. Once when she tried pulling on her shoes . . ."

Rachel felt the jolt from Elliot's hands as he grasped her by the shoulders. She saw her own long dark hair reflected in his bright eyes.

"This has nothing to do with bunions, Rachel. 'Lovely feet' is just an expression. The people who came down from the mountain—Armut's people—were Noah and his family."

Rachel studied him curiously. "I think your brain has been flooded for forty days."

"After the flood the ark came to rest somewhere up here, in the mountains of Ararat. But no one knows where, exactly." He curled up his lips and bounced his eyebrows up and down. "Until now."

"You're outrageous," Rachel declared. "Noah and his lot are just like Armut's donkeys and snakes—campfire chatter. All you'll find up in those mountains is snow, rocks, stinking goats, and maybe a mad sheepdog or two. And I have my doubts about the sheepdogs." "Dogs large enough to rip a man in half with a single shake of their jowls," Armut had told them. Ha!

"I'm still puzzled by one thing," Elliot said.

"*You?* Puzzled?" Rachel tried to sound as rude as possible. "I didn't know anything puzzled the Great and Powerful Elliot, Mr. Message Decoder."

"Look at the end of the tablet," he said, handing it to Rachel for her to examine. He leaned back, crossed his arms, and waited for a moment. "So, Rachel Ashton, Archeologist Extraordinaire and Campfire Story Critic, what do you make of that?"

Rachel glanced at the bottom of the clay tablet below all of the cuneiform writing. Two squiggly shapes, looking almost like a child's drawing, had been carved into the clay.

"It's original," Elliot added. "I mean, it was etched into the wet clay at the same time as the rest of the writing. But none of Dad's books talks about this symbol. It sure isn't cuneiform. I've never seen anything like it."

Something about the curving lines of the drawing seemed eerily familiar. They made Rachel feel uneasy, almost frightened. She looked closer. One of the smooth markings formed a shape resembling a bird or maybe a boat. The other one hung above the first. It was round with lines coming from it, like a picture-book sun in a cloudless sky. Suddenly a tingle of goose-bumps popped out all over her skin.

"I've seen this," shuddered Rachel.

"Where?" said a startled Elliot.

"Hanging below a scraggly old beard on a leather strap," she replied, wishing she could run from the memory. She felt a second crop of goosebumps sprout on her arms. "This is the picture on Old Tuz's neck-lace. Part of this sun thing along the top was missing. Broken off, I think. Otherwise, the picture is the same."

Carefully, she ran her fingertips across the clay drawing. Everything came back to her in a flash—the teahouse, the smell of coffee, Old Tuz's breath, suspicious Mr. Zebra Pants—everything.

"You're sure? You're sure you saw it on his necklace?" Elliot asked excitedly.

"Believe me, I got a much closer look than I wanted." Rachel pictured the dark necklace in her mind, swinging back and forth above her forehead from Old Tuz's dirty neck.

Elliot had already tugged his hooded sweatshirt over his head and trimmed the lamp.

"What are you doing?" Rachel questioned him.

"You said Old Tuz saw something up on the mountain, right?"

"But I told you . . . he's blind. And probably crazy!" Rachel yelled after a rapidly disappearing Elliot.

Elliot glanced back over his shoulder at her.

"I'm going to get Yedi," he grinned. "You and I have a date with a crazy man."

CHAPTER 8

The morning ride to Dog Biscuit had been a pleasant one. Rachel had begun to get the feel of traveling on horseback. For starters, she made sure Armut loosened her stirrups and cinched up the saddle properly on her lard-bellied mare. And, with three days between rides, her saddle sores had healed a bit.

Yedi seemed eager to take them back for a visit with Old Tuz. Almost too eager, as far as Rachel was concerned. He retraced the riding path from the dig back toward the city, adding a small detour that gave them a closer look at the crumbling Saray Palace. Rachel hoped it would be a snooping detour, but Yedi chickened out as usual. Oh well, at least he had convinced Armut to allow the three of them to return to Dog Biscuit alone. That was a start.

"You're enjoying this trip back to find that old Kurd, aren't you, you old snoop?" Rachel called out to Yedi over the jingle of the bells on his saddle.

"What is an 'old Snoopy'?" Yedi wondered.

"Not Snoopy," chirped Rachel. "Snoop. A snoop is . . ."

"A snoop is a busybody who sticks her nose into everyone else's business," Elliot butted in. "Like Rachel." He pulled his hat snug to block the sun.

"There are different types of snoops," Rachel offered in her most pompous voice, jumping at the chance to taunt Elliot. "Uncle Mason, for example. He's a snoop—a scientific snoop. He snoops through dead people's things."

"He's an archeologist, for Pete's sake!" defended Elliot.

Rachel wagged her finger at him. "But he's *still* a snoop."

She was doing her best to hide her nervousness. But as they guided their horses close to the dingy streets and hovels of Dog Biscuit, Rachel began to feel uneasy. Her skin tingled. All of this business about Noah's ark—the tablet, Armut's stories, Old Tuz and his broken necklace—it had to be more than just coincidence. An adventure lurked beneath it all. This could be her biggest snoop of all. Rachel could almost reach out and touch it.

Old Tuz lived near the outskirts of Dog Biscuit in a small, single-story shanty. It was one of a dozen run-down buildings that made up a squatters' village, surrounded by nothing more than dust and wind. Wooden beams, rotted by years of relentless sun and winter rains, jutted from beneath the flat, makeshift roofs. Patches of orange plaster lay scattered about the unpainted doors like strips of orange rind peeled from the outside walls. Behind the shacks stood a wooden structure with a leaky water spigot poking out one side. With a shock, Rachel realized this was the only bathroom for all the people in the area. It had the privacy of a movie theater.

Nearing the lonely cluster of shanty houses, Rachel saw two men step into the street, directly in their path. As they drew closer, the men grew familiar. There was no mistaking their clothing. It was Mr. Zebra Pants and his sidekick, Towel Head. Walking toward the teahouse, no doubt. Rachel wished she could go with them rather than face Old Tuz again.

Zebra Pants raised one hand, half waving, half cautioning them to stop. A smile of recognition snaked its way across his face as they met.

"So, young ones, what brings you back to Dogubeyazit?" he asked.

Yedi guided his horse forward, placing it in front of Rachel and Elliot, between them and the two men. He kept one arm twisted behind his back and flashed a signal to Rachel to stay put.

"We have need of a few things," Yedi said, avoiding the question.

*That's a dumb answer,* Rachel thought. *Why not tell them we're looking for Old Tuz? Perhaps they can tell us where to find him.*

Zebra Pants' tight smile faded a bit. He flipped his head in the direction of downtown Dog Biscuit, several blocks away.

"I am certain the downtown markets have all that you might need." His tone indicated suspicion rather than friendly advice. That's when Rachel noticed something she hadn't seen before. From her horseback view, she saw a small block of metal poking from the waistband of Zebra Pants' pants. Like other Kurds she had met, he kept his hands lively and expressive when he spoke. But when he remained silent, his right hand always rested within centimeters of the dull metal rectangle, and his index finger tapped against it like a ticking clock.

"I am certain we will stop at the market before we return to the dig site," Yedi replied, holding his ground.

"Ahmet and I are on our way there now. Perhaps we can help you load your supplies so you can be on your way?"

Yedi nodded a respectful thank-you. "It is kind of you to offer. But we will not trouble you." He nodded again, ending the conversation.

Zebra Pants flashed them a long threatening stare. His yellow eyes were those of the snake in Armut's campfire story, only smaller and beadier. The snake eyes moved from Yedi to Elliot, finally coming to rest on Rachel.

"Do not tarry long in the city," he warned them. "Curious children have a way of finding trouble."

He beckoned to Towel Head, and the pair slithered along the dusty street toward the teahouse, fading into the flat-roofed shadows like ghosts.

"What was *that* all about?" huffed Rachel.

"Sounded like a threat to me," said Elliot.

"We should avoid them in the future," came Yedi's reply. He urged his horse forward.

"Avoid them?" Rachel felt indignant. "I'd like to pop

them one! How rude! Who do they think they are?"

"I don't know." Elliot seemed serious. "I do know that popping them would not be wise. The guy in the striped pants had a pistol tucked into his pants."

"That was a *gun*?" Rachel gasped.

"Yes," Yedi interjected. "Those men are fighters in a war against the government. They are not happy with the ways of Turkey. They hope to change them."

"Kurdish freedom fighters?" Elliot asked. Yedi nodded. He was right, of course. Rachel knew he would be. He looked at her and must have noticed her sour glare. "I've read about them," he said, shrugging his shoulders and smiling weakly.

"But their ideas of freedom are not always best for the Kurdish people, not even for those who have escaped to the mountains and live where the government cannot see them," explained Yedi. "Sometimes their ideas bring much trouble to our people."

Yedi led them past two or three shacks until they reached one where a feeble figure sat limply on a stool near the door. After tying his horse to a broken fence nearby, Yedi crossed into the shadow of the small overhanging roof above the figure. A butterfly flew up from Rachel's stomach and caught in her throat. Old Tuz.

Yedi greeted him in Kurdish. Old Tuz rattled off a mouthful of gibberish in reply, and Yedi respectfully bobbed his head up and down as Old Tuz spoke, even though the old man couldn't see a thing.

*That's it,* Rachel thought. *I'm tired of all of this gibberish business.* Butterfly or not, she cleared her throat and pushed her voice through her fear.

"Wait a minute," she said, quickly tying her horse and taking one step closer to the white-haired Kurd. "I know you speak English. I heard you, at the teahouse."

Old Tuz tilted his head in her direction. One milky eye fixated on her. A grin exposed his yellow-stained teeth.

"Ahhh. The young girl from the teahouse."

"See?" Rachel threw both hands in the air. "He speaks English. Zebra Pants and his buddy with the towel wrapped around his head speak English too. *Everybody* speaks English. But no one will admit it."

"There is an old Turkish proverb," Old Tuz replied in a raspy voice. "'Even from a crooked chimney, the smoke rises straight.' Do not trust everyone you meet here in the mountains. Do not believe all that you are told, for not everyone can be trusted."

"Like Zebra Pants and Towel Head," Rachel muttered to Elliot.

Old Tuz paused to grope for Yedi's hands. "Yedi and his apo, they are my trusted friends."

"Thank you, Effendi," Yedi answered, squeezing the Kurd's gnarled fingers in his own. "I would like very much for you to meet my trusted friends, Rachel and Elliot."

Elliot shook Old Tuz's hand carefully. Rachel, however, couldn't bring herself to get within an arm's length of him. Besides, she suddenly felt a bit awkward knowing that Yedi considered her a trusted friend. Most of her friends were a lot like her—not terribly trustworthy.

Instead of shaking hands, she asked, "How do we know you're really blind?"

"Rachel!" Elliot said with a stern look, motioning his hand as if to shush her.

Old Tuz's grin returned. "You learn quickly, Young Wise One. You are testing whether this old man's smoke comes from a straight chimney. I am quite blind, I assure you."

"Young Wise One." Rachel liked the sound of that. Especially when someone said it to her and not to Elliot.

"We have come to ask you about the mountain," Yedi began.

Old Tuz's eyes seemed to brighten.

"Uh, Mr. Tuz," Elliot said hesitantly. "Yedi found a very old clay tablet, up near the monastery. Do you know where that is?"

"Yes, I have been on the mountain many times," he replied.

"Well, I've decoded the message written on the tablet. It's a map of some sort, almost like a treasure map. Rachel says you have seen . . ." Elliot adjusted his glasses and peered closer at the milky eyes before him. "I mean, she says you know of something hidden up there. We were wondering . . ."

"It is there," Old Tuz interrupted, in a familiar voice that sent chills down Rachel's neck. "Hidden by the hand of God."

Elliot turned to Yedi and shrugged his shoulders.

"What is there, Effendi Tuz?" Yedi persisted.

"The great ship of Nu-Wah. I have touched it, with my own hands." Old Tuz fumbled beneath the collar of his soiled shirt for a moment. The wooden amulet appeared in his hands, attached to the leather strap around his neck. He turned it slowly in his fingers, feeling every groove of the carved wood.

Rachel inched closer for a better look at the necklace. Sure enough, the boatlike design hung there, just as she remembered. Elliot looked at her over his shoulder.

"That's it," he uttered. Rachel felt herself nod.

"Can you tell us about your visit to the great ship?" asked Yedi.

"It was a long time ago," the old man replied slowly. He gripped the amulet and looked blankly toward the ground. "I was just a boy. My father took me to the mountain, just as his father had taken him. We packed food on our donkey and camped with shepherds grazing their sheep on the mountainside. I have never seen summer pastures so green as those of Ararat."

"How could you see them?" Elliot had to ask.

"I have not always had eyes of milk. My eyes were as sharp as daggers then." Old Tuz shifted on his stool. "My father led us near the monastery. He told me the story of the great earthquake that destroyed it. Then we left the donkey and climbed a narrow path until stones cluttered our way and the rocks turned an angry gray. Suddenly a door in the mountain opened and swallowed us. A mighty river rushed beside us and the air smelled sweet of cedar trees. My father removed his cloak, for it was warm inside the mountain."

Old Tuz spread both arms and lightly wiggled his fingers. "A thousand tiny golden stars twinkled around us, and yet the sun shone upon us, for it was daylight. And there, where night and day meet inside the mountain, was the great ship."

Rachel felt all hopes of adventure melting away. Just as she had suspected, Old Tuz was a rambling old fossil, crazy as a doodlebug. According to him, finding Noah's ark was a breeze: just ride a donkey down the mountain's throat until you come to the place where the stars shine all day long. Take a right and you're there. No problem. She could make that trip and still be home in time to skin a goat for supper.

The old Kurd stood up. "The giant ship rested inside the mountain and on its top lay a pasture greener than Ararat itself."

"Were there windows? Could you see inside?" Elliot wondered.

"Tiny windows. On the roof." Old Tuz nodded his head weakly as he spoke. "We walked into its belly through a large opening in its side."

"You went *in* it?" Elliot sputtered. Rachel thought his eyeballs would drop from his head.

"Oh, yes. Yes. We walked through the rooms and I placed my hands on the black wood. Then my father took me up the stairs. We crawled onto the top and looked down into a valley that had no bottom. He said to me, 'This is the great ship of Ararat. I show it to you, just as your grandfather showed it to me, and his father before him. And you shall show it to your sons. It is a jewel, hidden in the rocks by God since time began.'

"We crawled back inside the ship and he led me to

the opening. Several small pieces of the black wood lay on the floor. My father put one in his cloak." Old Tuz pressed the amulet to his chest. "Soon it was foggy. I was very tired. I slept on the donkey all the way back to the city."

"My friends and I would very much like to see the great ship, just as you have," Yedi said.

"Maybe one of your sons could take us there, or at least show us the way," Elliot suggested.

Old Tuz was slow to answer. "I have no sons. And both of my daughters died with virus long ago. They never saw the ship."

Rachel's stomach tightened into a lump. Maybe that's why this old man had taken special interest in her—she reminded him of the daughters he had lost.

Old Tuz stepped backward several paces and felt for his stool behind him. Then he bent his knobby knees and sat.

"Is there anyone who can point us to this place you have spoken of?" Yedi seemed to be reading Elliot's mind and asking all the right questions.

"I do not think so." He paused. "But you will find it."

Startled, Elliot jumped a little. Now it was Old Tuz who was reading minds, and predicting the future as well. How could he know the outcome of their search?

"The mountain can be dangerous. Sometimes it becomes angry," he warned them.

After a brief silence, Yedi said something in gibberish and motioned to Rachel and Elliot that it was time to go. When they turned to leave, the raspy voice reached out to Rachel a final time.

"Young Wise One . . ."

Rachel spun around. "Me?"

He nodded, beckoning to her with one crooked finger. She approached him warily, determined not to be afraid.

"Young Wise One . . ." he said again in a whisper. "Beware of snakes."

"On the mountain?"

"On the mountain," he said, staring directly into her eyes. "And in the city."

Rachel stepped closer and pressed her face centimeters away from his. Then she backed away and waved a hand back and forth in front of his eyes. Nothing. Blind as a cavefish.

They stepped away from Old Tuz's flat-roofed shack. Several hours of daylight remained, enough to get them to the market and safely back to the dig site. Yedi lingered for a moment, telling the aged Kurd good-bye while Elliot untied the horses.

As soon as they were mounted and on their way, Elliot turned to Rachel.

"Young Wise One?"

Yedi giggled.

Rachel felt herself sit a little taller in her saddle. "You know, I still say he's crazy as a loon. But I'm beginning to like that old Kurd."

# CHAPTER 9

Yedi seemed especially quiet on the ride back from
Dog Biscuit. He didn't take any detours and he ignored
Rachel's small talk with Elliot. At one point, with darkness falling on the mountain and the dig site still a
quarter mile away, he lifted the bells from his saddle
and muffled them in his riding blanket.

"What are you doing?" Rachel asked. "I've come to
like that little jingle of yours. It makes me think of you
as a snoopy Santa Claus."

Yedi refused to answer. Instead, he looked nervously
around and urged his horse into a slow trot. "You must
hurry also," was all he said. He didn't stop until they
had safely reached the wooden lean-to that served as a
stable at the dig.

"Who put the bee in your baggy pants?" Rachel
called to him as she tethered her horse to the stable
wall. Still no answer. So she turned to Elliot. "Well,"
she said coarsely, loud enough for Yedi to overhear, "I
think he hurried us back here because Armut is making goat sandwiches for dinner. Again."

Yedi worked quickly, shoveling several armloads of hay for the horses. Then he stopped and listened to the faint sound of chirping crickets floating on the mountain breeze.

"What's the matter, Yedi?" Elliot asked.

"I have the feeling that someone has followed us," he said at last, his dark eyes darting back and forth.

"Who?"

"I am not certain. There are bandits along the roads, outside of the city. Travelers must always be cautious." He relaxed a little. "It is probably nothing."

He moved closer to help Elliot unload supplies from the horses.

"Please take these supplies to Apo and Effendi Mason," he directed.

"What do you think you're going to do?" Rachel challenged.

"I will stay here and watch the horses, until they are fed."

"Suit yourself," grumped Rachel.

"I'm staying too," Elliot joined in. "Tell Dad where we are, okay, Rachel?"

"Oh, alright." Rachel sighed openly and made loud grunting sounds as she picked up the two bags of supplies. She was hoping for sympathy, having to carry everything herself. Then a disturbing thought struck her.

"Wait a minute," she said, turning back toward the boys. "If bandits followed us here, then why am I walking from the stable to the work tent *alone*? In the dark?" She stuck her nose in the air and waited for an answer.

Elliot and Yedi exchanged glances. Yedi shrugged. Elliot rose to his feet.

"I'll go with you, Young Wise One." He laughed light-heartedly, then looked squarely at Yedi. "You'll be fine?" he asked him.

"Yes. I will come in a moment," Yedi replied.

"Here," Rachel huffed, shoving both bags of supplies into Elliot's arms. "You carry these. I'll watch for bandits."

"Don't worry about me, Yedi. I'm walking with the Young Wise One," joked Elliot.

"And stop calling me that!" Rachel yelled, loud enough to scare away any bandits lurking around the camp.

They left the stable and walked past the small campfire toward the glowing lanterns of the work tent. Rachel didn't see any bandits. And from Yedi's behavior, she questioned whether he was telling them everything he knew.

Inside the tent, Uncle Mason and Armut huddled around a lantern on the dirt-covered worktable. They had stumbled onto a couple of artifacts earlier in the day, buried in a shallow sinkhole near the base of a stone pillar. One was a badly dented gold cup, over which they (and Elliot) made quite a fuss. The other was a short, stocky figurine carved from black stone—as heavy as it was ugly. The figurine had a wavy beard and wide, hollow eyes. It reminded Rachel of Old Tuz.

"Classic Urartian craftsmanship," Uncle Mason must have said a hundred times, rubbing his hand around the rim of the gold cup as if expecting a genie to pop out. "Goodness Agnes! What do you think, Armut? Good enough for the museum in Van?"

"Oh, yes. I will contact the museum curator next week and make the arrangements," said Armut.

"You've got to be joking," Rachel said, grabbing the figurine. "You came all the way across the world to find this ugly statue, just to leave it here in some museum?"

"I'm afraid so, Rachel," Uncle Mason said with a hint of disappointment. "Most governments allow archeologists to dig with the understanding that anything they find must stay in that country. These artifacts belong to the people of Turkey."

"Finders, keepers, I say," huffed Rachel. She handed the statue to Armut, who carefully tied an identification tag around each artifact and placed them in the SIMA travel trunk for safekeeping.

"Your trip to the city . . . how was it?" Armut asked.

"Great," Elliot jumped in, before Rachel could answer. "We got everything we needed. No problems."

"Excuse me," Rachel said rudely, preparing to correct him. "No problems? Maybe you and I went on different trips today." She didn't know where to begin—with Old Tuz, with Zebra Pants and Towel Head, or maybe with Yedi's vanishing bandits that almost ambushed them on the road home. "For starters, Yedi thinks we were—"

A warning poke in the ribs from Elliot's finger stopped her in midsentence. The worried look on Armut's face told her that any mention of problems might mean the end of their travels alone. So she forced a weak smile.

"Uh . . . Yedi thought we would be late for supper."

"Supper!" The look on Armut's face quickly changed from worry to alarm. "My stew!" he cried. "I nearly forgot." He bounded from the tent toward the campfire.

Uncle Mason laughed. "I guess it's dinnertime," he said, following Armut.

As soon as Uncle Mason left the tent, Rachel whirled around to face Elliot and rubbed her ribs.

"What's the big idea, stabbing my ribs like that? I could be injured. I could be bleeding internally!"

"Relax, Rachel. You'll survive," Elliot said. "I plan to tell Dad about our visit to Old Tuz. This just wasn't the right time to explain it."

Rachel maintained her scowl. "There aren't any doctors out here in this wilderness," she began her threat.

"Wilderness? We're three miles from the city, for Pete's sake!"

"What if I were really hurt? Cracked ribs or something? Then what?"

"Well," Elliot said thoughtfully, "I guess we would give you a bandage from the first-aid kit and call you *Dr.* Young Wise One."

"You're disgusting," she fumed.

"Thanks," he replied, grabbing his jacket and pulling back the tent flap. He smiled. "Speaking of disgusting, . . . let's go eat some of Armut's goat."

"Yuk." Rachel wasn't particularly hungry, but she slipped into her jacket and followed him anyway.

Yedi was waiting at the campfire, helping Armut dish out generous portions of overcooked stew. Rachel sat cross-legged near the large platter of crusty bread that would be her supper. Yedi knew better than to offer her stew.

After a few minutes of small talk about that dreadfully ugly figurine and the museum in Van, the circle grew quiet. Yedi and Elliot exchanged a knowing glance. Then Yedi cleared his throat.

"Effendi Mason," he began, "you will be leaving in a few days, yes?"

"Three days, to be exact," Uncle Mason replied between bites of stew. "Unless Mehlat and his plane decide to leave early."

"I would very much like to take my new friends, Elliot and Rachel, to visit a *yaila* before they must leave Turkey."

"Who on earth is A-yea-lah?" Rachel asked. She caught Elliot staring at her out of the corner of his eye.

"A *yaila* isn't a who," Uncle Mason responded. "It's a Kurdish summer camp. Families take their livestock to pasture on the mountainside during the short summer months and stay at a yaila."

"Apo's friend Selik has a yaila near the saddle of the mountain. It is only an hour's ride from here," said Yedi. He looked at Rachel pointedly. "Maybe two hours."

"Funny," Rachel snarled back.

"It is an easy ride to the camp," Yedi persisted.

Rachel noticed Elliot nodding heartily in agreement. Then a light clicked on in her young, wise brain. Yedi had been scheming a way to get them up on the mountain, closer to the ark. And Elliot was in on the plan. Visiting a summer camp—what a perfect excuse! Oh, this was classy. Yedi the Snoop had outdone himself this time. He had even fooled her, for a minute.

Uncle Mason thought for a long while, tediously coiling a slice of bread around a strip of charred goat meat. He usually appreciated a sense of adventure. But Yedi's request appeared to carry some serious overtones. Finally he looked to Armut for advice.

"What do you think, Armut?"

Armut furrowed his brow and pursed his lips. Rachel recognized the look on his face as one that always came before the word "no." She had to say something before Armut nixed the idea.

"I went to summer camp in Great Britain," she offered. "Twice, in fact. The second time I helped the camp counselors with flag duty and so forth. My camp experience might be helpful, even for just a day."

Elliot's eyes rolled in his head. A small smile widened Armut's full face. Slowly the smile grew into a grin, then a chuckle, and finally blossomed into a rolling belly laugh.

Rachel felt her face flush.

"What's so funny?" she snapped.

"Perhaps a climb to the yaila would be a good learning experience after all," Armut said, finishing his laugh at her expense. "You may find the Kurdish camp quite different from that of your childhood. And I am certain Selik would welcome a visit."

Yedi brightened. "Good!" he exclaimed. "We will leave early tomorrow and return at nightfall."

Armut's smile faded and he held a serious finger in the air. "Return by sunset," he declared.

"By sunset, Apo," Yedi confirmed. He slunk a smile at Elliot and winked slyly at Rachel.

# CHAPTER 10

Rachel didn't sleep well. Her dreams overflowed with images of skinny zebras with yellow eyes, carrying guns, jumping over the ugly black figurine Uncle Mason had unearthed. She much preferred counting sheep. Even counting goats would have been better.

When Elliot woke her at dawn, she felt confused and exhausted, as if night had never come.

"Yedi is waiting," Elliot said softly. "We need an early start, so we can watch for the shadow on the mountain." His crudely drawn ark map poked from the pocket of his jacket.

Rachel rose to her feet like a zombie and fumbled for her shoes and jacket.

"Another morning, another saddle sore," she mumbled.

Elliot waited impatiently outside the tent. "Come on!" he called in a loud whisper.

"Alright, alright!" Rachel trudged out to the stable, where Armut and Yedi awaited them in the pale light of sunrise. They had already watered and saddled the horses. Rachel mounted her mare, barely noticing the cold morning air.

"Travel with great care," Armut told them. "May your journey be steadily upward."

"What's that supposed to mean?" Rachel grumbled.

"It is an old Kurdish blessing. It means 'Do not fall off the mountain,'" Yedi translated.

He led them northeast up a broad, gentle slope formed by the saddle of rock connecting Greater and Lesser Ararat. According to Elliot, Mr. Turkish Geography, a dark glacier lay on the other side of the saddle, and beneath it lay the remains of the old monastery. And somewhere, around the crest of the saddle, lay Noah's ark.

As they climbed, the green pastures gradually gave way to scruffy grass, and the frequent clumps of color-ful wildflowers became few and sparse. Rachel felt woozy and short of breath as their ascent led them into thinning mountain air. Finally, after nearly an hour, the climb steepened abruptly. The broad path became little more than a sheep trail, making it impossible to follow on horseback. So the trio dismounted, and at Yedi's bidding, they continued on foot, leading the horses. Soon the path curved around a rocky outcropping and opened onto a broad plateau of gray boulders dotted with a few scrubby trees. Flat and open, the plateau was rimmed by mountain slopes on two sides, giving way to lush grazing pastures to the south.

Beautiful as they were, Rachel had grown weary of the blue-green mountains, stretches of green pasture, and pale purple haze hanging in the air around them.

Her horse had no desire to climb farther. Neither did she. And she was tired of prodding and coaxing the dumpy mare up the winding path.

"Stubborn animal!" Rachel snapped at her horse. "If I didn't know better, I would swear you were a mule!"

"That horse probably says the same thing about you," Elliot said casually.

Rachel ignored Mr. Smart Mouth for now, turning her frustration to Yedi.

"Where is this stupid shepherd camp of yours, anyway? We should have reached it hours ago. Besides, it's colder up here than at the dig."

The jingling bells on Yedi's saddle fell silent as his horse came to a halt.

"It is no further. We are here," he said.

Rachel searched the hazy slopes and pastures for the slightest sign of a camp. She saw nothing—no playground, no mess hall, no bunkhouses . . . absolutely nothing. Not even a flagpole. They had ridden halfway up the mountain for nothing.

She didn't know whether to pout or scream. Instead, she flopped onto a flattened rock and began peeling another layer of skin from the tip of her sunburned nose, like a lizard shedding her skin.

Almost like magic, a stocky man in baggy pants stepped from behind a low cluster of boulders and extended his arms toward Rachel.

Startled, Rachel leaped to her feet. She clutched instinctively at her jacket pockets, hoping to fish out anything she could use as a weapon.

"S-stay back," she stammered. "Stay back or I'll . . .

I'll . . ." Her hand found something hard and round in her left-hand pocket and she jerked it out with convincing courage. It was a stale piece of bread, left over from Armut's goat feast the night before.

"Or you'll what, Rachel?" Elliot posed. "Or you'll make him a bologna sandwich?"

Yedi waved and greeted the man in gibberish. Kurdish, actually. The man tugged at his hat and beckoned to them to come.

A sudden rush of relief came over Rachel. She felt her shoulders slump.

"Selik, I presume?" she said, turning to Yedi.

Yedi nodded. Slowly, he led his horse to meet the man, who smiled as they approached. The man pointed toward a low rise about fifty yards ahead, where a scattering of brightly colored makeshift tents, rock shelters, skirt-clad women, children, sheep, chickens, and a glowing campfire awaited them. This was hardly the camp Rachel had imagined. The only thing resembling a flagpole was a twisted tree draped in a wide bolt of orange cloth—and the only thing saluting it was a sheep.

Soon two more men in baggy pants joined Selik.

"They will care for our horses," said Yedi, passing the reins to one of the men. "We should warm ourselves by the fire."

As they crossed the yaila, passing tents and clusters of women and children washing plastic tubs and metal pots, Rachel pondered everything she saw—the people and the harsh conditions under which they lived. Finally she just had to ask.

"Where is the rest of the camp? You know, the main building, the Activity Director's quarters, the mess hall?"

Yedi fixed his eyes on her curiously.

"This is it, Rachel," Elliot said. "You were expecting maybe a vacation resort for the rich and famous? These people endure this place for the good of their livestock." He squinted against the cold breeze that had begun to whistle down from the barren summit far above them.

"There are certain things you should know," said Yedi, still somewhat puzzled by Rachel's expectations. "Selik's people do not speak English. If you are offered gifts or food, take them with thanks."

Rachel heard only part of Yedi's advice. She was too busy watching several large dogs trotting around the perimeter of the camp, constantly moving, like sentries keeping vigil. They weaved in and out between the wheels of an old wooden donkey cart used for hauling supplies, parked at the camp's edge. Yedi nodded at the dogs cautiously, as if reading Rachel's mind.

"And it is best to avoid the Anatolians," he suggested.

"The who?"

"The dogs," came Yedi's reply. "To them we are strangers."

"They're native dogs," Elliot explained. "The shepherds keep them to fight off animals that snatch away sheep—like bears and wolves. They can be meaner than dirt."

A large, inviting fire blazed at the center of the yaila. When they reached it, Rachel stretched her fingers toward it. Gradually, they tingled to life again as she placed them next to its radiant heat.

"Now *this* is a fire," Rachel said. "Unlike those we've had at *our* campsite."

"Are you suggesting Yedi and I don't know how to build fires?" bantered Elliot.

"You two wouldn't know a good fire if it leaped up and singed off your eyebrows! Why haven't you made us a campfire like this one?"

At that moment, a middle-aged Kurdish woman wearing three or four sets of skirts approached the fire, carrying a canvas bag over her shoulder. Squatting and opening the bag, she reached in and plucked out several dozen brown, irregular pats, which she threw carelessly into the flames.

"Looks like we need some firestarters, like these," Elliot observed. He picked one from the bag and tossed it in Rachel's direction. She bobbled it but managed to hold on.

"Where do we get them?" she asked.

"Easy," Elliot said, swapping smiles with Yedi. "You stand behind a sheep. And wait."

"You're disgusting, both of you!" She threw the sheep dropping back at Elliot. He dodged it easily. Then he slipped his crumpled ark map from his pocket, uncrumpled it, and studied the notes he had made. Rachel moved closer to peer over his shoulder.

"Okay. I figure we're situated somewhere around here," he noted, his finger circling an area on his map partway up the saddle between the mountain summits. He checked his watch. "Nine o'clock." He braced his back to the wind and faced east. "Not a cloud in the sky, and a perfect shadow falling our way from Lesser Ararat." Wrinkles of disappointment formed on his forehead, partly hidden under his hat's brim. "I don't get it."

"What is wrong?" asked Yedi.

"The shadow—it's too short. It doesn't reach all the way to Greater Ararat. It barely reaches across the saddle."

Rachel shivered a bit in the brisk wind. Elliot wasn't one to give up easily. The simple fact that their map was now worthless and the wind had turned cool wouldn't be enough to discourage his logical, although sometimes irritating, brain. She wasn't ready to give up, either.

"Now what?" she challenged.

"The message on the clay tablet said 'the shadow points the way,'" he reviewed aloud. He stared thoughtfully at the dark triangular shadow cast by the smaller mountain. Its tip came to a sharp point along the saddle's ridge, forming a long arrow directed straight up the mountainside. "What's up there, Yedi, above the camp?"

"I do not know. I have rarely gone above the yaila."

"We'll rest an hour, then hike up as far as we can go, until we run out of easy footing. We should be able to climb another half mile without much problem." The gleam returned to Elliot's eyes.

"To reach the dig site before sunset, we must leave the yaila by four o'clock," Yedi reminded him. Elliot shivered out a nod. A short burst of wind whipped through the camp.

"Are we done here?" Rachel squawked. She really hadn't dressed for the chilly mountain. "Could we possibly crawl into one of these tents, or shelters, or whatever they are, before my toes drop off?"

Before she could utter another word, two young women, twittering gibberish, whisked Rachel off to a stone shelter formed by several big rock formations rising from the pebbled soil. Rachel was surprised at how warm the shelter felt, blocking the path of the chilling wind. One woman wrapped her in a colorful red blanket into which a large zigzag design of sheep's wool had been woven. The other woman left the shelter and walked toward the center of the camp, shooing four or five scrawny chickens out of her way and sending them squawking and flapping madly. She soon returned, carrying a bowl of dark stew, bread, a cup of thick white stuff, and a block of cheese that smelled like rotting gym socks.

"Ugh!" Rachel whined. "I see you and Armut use the same cookbook."

The women giggled politely.

"You don't understand a word I'm saying, do you?"

Their blank faces smiled in reply.

"I gave up two weeks of tennis lessons to come here. Did you know that? Of course you didn't know that. And you still don't," Rachel sighed. She looked out over the yaila with a critical eye. "This camp of yours isn't a bad start. You could build a mess hall around that central campfire spot, maybe put a flagpole out in front, and hire a camp counselor."

The women's eyes remained fixed on her. Suddenly

Rachel remembered the plane ride with Mehlat and the kind, toothless woman. Fumbling in her pocket, she pulled out the colorful scarf the old Kurdish woman had given her. She draped it over her hair and tied it neatly beneath her chin. The women clapped and giggled.

"There," Rachel said. "Now we have something in common. We look alike." She peered closer at the women. "Well, sort of."

The woman who had braved the chickens to get Rachel's meal pushed the steaming stew bowl closer.

"Oh, lovely. Goat stew—my favorite. How did you know?"

Both women waited anxiously for Rachel to eat.

"Sorry, I believe I'll pass on the stew. Watching my weight, you know. I suppose I should taste something so as not to appear rude," she said aloud. She pointed to the cup of thick white stuff. "That looks safe enough. Maybe I'll try some."

The Chicken Woman quickly found her a spoon.

"A spoon," Rachel said sheepishly. "Actually, I rather hoped you wouldn't find one." She sniffed the cup. It smelled like *sweet* rotting gym socks.

"*Buyurun, buyurun,*" said Chicken Woman.

"Right. Whatever you say." Rachel puckered, closed her eyes, and forced the first pitiful spoonful past her lips. It tasted sweet and creamy, yet had a bite to it.

"Mmm. Not bad," she said, surprised. She scooped herself a second spoonful and settled back against the protective rock shelter.

"So . . . seen any good movies lately?" Rachel couldn't

help but laugh at her ridiculous situation, sitting in a rock pile two miles up a mountain with a couple of goat-herds who couldn't understand a word she spoke.

"No?" she went on. "I suppose not. I imagine you simply wait for the videos to be delivered by mules." Rachel laughed again. So did the women. She had their full attention. "You like that one?" she said, sounding like a stand-up comic. "I've got a million of them. Have you heard the one about the two wild dogs, the shepherd, and the lightning bolt?"

Moments later, Elliot appeared in front of the rock shelter. Tipping the brim of his safari hat to the women, he smiled shyly.

"*Merhaba*," he said in Turkish.

The women looked at one another, giggled and bubbled over until Rachel feared their skirts would pop right off their hips.

"You speak Turkey now, I suppose?" Rachel said to him. "Let me guess . . . you did a little reading in the past hour and picked up a whole new language, right?"

"Just telling your hosts 'hello.' I hate to break up this tea party, ladies," Elliot said, adjusting his glasses, "but we're burning daylight. The mountain waits for no one."

"Kind of like you and Yedi," snooted Rachel. She turned to each of her full-skirted hosts and shrugged her shoulders.

"Pea Brain is here. Gotta go. It's been lovely. Oh, save this white stuff for me, would you?" She shoved the cup and spoon to the Chicken Woman.

"Nice scarf, Rachel," Elliot commented. Rachel

immediately jerked it from her head. She had forgotten all about it. "It's a nice touch—it goes well with the goat yogurt."

"The *what*?"

Elliot pointed to the creamy white blob on her spoon. "Goat yogurt. Great stuff. Made fresh, right here at Yaila Farms."

Rachel's tongue crawled its way out through her lips. "Yuk! Why didn't someone tell me?"

"You probably never asked. Now come on."

Rachel nodded a final thank-you to her hosts, just as Yedi had instructed. Then, like a conductor priming an orchestra, she raised her arms and commanded the two women.

"Repeat after me . . . say, 'Good-bye, Pea Brain.'"

The women waved coyly at Elliot. In broken English they called out to him, right on cue, "Good-bye, Pea Brain."

Rachel laughed all the way to the edge of the camp, past the chickens and the dogs and the burning sheep dung. They stopped one last time at the campfire, where Yedi waited. But when she and Elliot headed up the slope beyond the camp, Yedi stopped at the old donkey cart.

"Well, aren't you coming, Snoopy?" Rachel inquired.

"No," answered Yedi. "I will stay behind."

"Why?"

He hesitated. "I will stay behind," he repeated. "You must go search for the great ship. But do not let the mountain trick you. If the slope becomes dangerous or the fog comes to rest upon you, you must turn back.

Now, go while the sun is high."

Yedi was a first-class snoop. It seemed odd to Rachel that he would choose to stay at the yaila. But he had smarts, and he probably had his reasons. If he considered Rachel his trusted friend, she would just have to trust him in return.

It wasn't long before Rachel began to feel the full effects of the high altitude. The slope ahead steepened once the yaila had disappeared behind them, and hiking became a chore. Her lungs ached for air. She felt light-headed and giddy. She climbed without thinking, moving in slow motion, barely noticing the loose rocks and brisk winds battling against them. Thirty minutes later, Elliot suggested they stop for a rest. Using a large pair of boulders as a windbreak, they squatted in the sunshine, facing Lesser Ararat. The smaller mountain's shadow had shortened as the sun rose higher, casting shade only on the far portion of the saddle of rock between the two peaks.

"We're on the right track," Elliot panted. He pointed to the tip of the shadow, which now aimed directly at them like a gigantic gray arrow. "I'm just not sure how much higher we need to go. Remember Ground Rule Two—'Keep your eyes and ears open.'"

Rachel was quickly finding it hard to remember anything. The altitude and the cold had zapped her energy and made her feel silly. She giggled for no reason at all, then giggled again because her laugh reminded her of Yedi's goofy giggle.

"Are you okay?" Elliot asked. "This air is awfully thin. It can make you dizzy."

She stood. "I am absolutely fine. Come on, Adventure King, we're burning daylight." She took the lead up the narrowing slope and giggled again at the sound of Elliot scrambling to keep up. Suddenly a blur of movement caught her bleary eyes. A furry blob loped across the open plateau behind them.

"Someone's following us," Rachel said. "Maybe Snoopy decided to come along after all."

Elliot stopped for a closer look. "That can't be Yedi—unless he's sprouted two extra legs and a lot of hair."

The furry object came into clearer view.

"Oh, look Elliot. It's a dog. I'll see if I can get him to come."

"I don't like the looks of that dog, Rachel," Elliot said.

"Oh, it's only one of those shepherd dogs. What did Yedi call them?"

"Anatolians," Elliot answered. "Just let him be."

"He's probably searching for a lost sheep or goat or something," Rachel said, not really listening. "Here doggie, doggie!" she yelled at the top of her burning lungs. The word 'doggie' bounced around the mountain walls in a circling echo. "C'mon, boy! Here doggie!"

"Rachel . . . ," Elliot repeated, his teeth clenched.

Ears flared, coat whipping in the mountain breeze, the furry creature turned and bounded across the gentle barren slope.

"That's it!" Rachel called cheerily. "C'mon, boy, that's it!" The dog came straight toward her voice. "See, I told you he was just searching for a lost shee—"

Suddenly she couldn't breathe. The collar of her jacket

clamped tightly around her neck, squeezing out her breath in short, squeaky bursts as Elliot yanked fiercely on her hood.

"Run, Rachel! Run!" Elliot was screaming in her ear.

The dog clipped across the rocky ground, halving the distance between them in moments. With a final jerk, Elliot let go of her jacket, toppling her backward. She struggled to her feet and fought to regain her balance on the slippery rock slope.

By now the dog had reached the near side of the glacial plateau, still in a dead run, less than a hundred meters below their perch. His muzzle curled into a permanent sneer lined with froth and fury. Elliot's voice rang out behind her.

"Hurry up! Hurry up!"

Fifty meters down the mountain the snarling dog gnashed his teeth and growled threateningly at the boulders hindering his climb. Rachel clambered over a ridge of black rock, trying to keep pace with Elliot. Just beyond the ridge, a steep, narrow path appeared. Elliot wedged himself at its base by pressing his back against one side of the rock wall, propping a foot on the opposite wall for support.

*Twenty-five meters away.* Rachel heard the dog's claws clicking madly, trying to gain a foothold on the gray mountain stone. She groped for Elliot's outstretched arm several times until her hand finally clamped around his wrist.

"Come on!" he urged.

Together they scrambled upward to the path's end, only to find a solid wall of rock and a narrow opening in the side of the mountain.

"There's no time!" Elliot yelled. "Jump in!"

He disappeared headfirst into the cave's mouth. Rachel followed him, diving headlong into the slit of blackness. Their escape route bought them five extra seconds—just enough time for each to grab a fistful of rocks.

An instant later the snarling Anatolian thrust his snout into their hideaway, his fierce jaws snapping inches from Rachel's face.

CHAPTER 11

"Now!" cried Elliot.

Rachel flung her rocks with all of her might. Elliot did the same. The dog rolled backward, sliding helplessly down the rock-strewn pathway. An eerie silence followed.

"He'll be back any minute," Elliot panted between breaths. "And next time, a pelting of rocks won't be enough. Here," he said, turning away from her, "grab the back of my jacket."

For once, Rachel did as she was told. No questions asked.

"Now, hold on."

Elliot stood and reached blindly into the darkness of the cave until his hands found a rock wall. He felt his way deeper into the frightening hole in the mountain, away from its opening, away from the jaws of the Anatolian. Obediently, Rachel shuffled behind him.

This was her fault. She knew that. She knew Elliot knew that too. But he wouldn't say so. Instead, he shuffled silently through the darkness, pulling her along behind him like a tow truck hauling a bashed-up car. Once, just once, she wished he would scream and holler at her. Then she would have good reason to be angry with him.

This seemed like a good time to apologize for getting them into this mess. She just couldn't bring herself to say it.

"Stupid dog!" she said angrily instead. "If . . . if . . ." Then, in the dark where she didn't have to look into Elliot's eyes, she forced herself to say the two words she hated most.

"Elliot . . . I'm sorry."

"It's okay," Elliot said hoarsely. "We'll stay in here for a minute. If the dog doesn't leave, we'll need to find another way out. And soon. In a few more hours we've got to climb back down to the camp."

He continued inching along the cave wall. The farther they went, the damper and darker the cave grew. The darkness didn't matter to Rachel, however. Her eyes were clamped shut, and she held one hand over her mouth just in case any bats tried to fly inside.

Several minutes passed before Rachel opened her eyes and looked back at the cave opening. It seemed dim and distant and appeared far below them, as did the faint barking of the angry Anatolian. Apparently the cave floor sloped upward into the mountain. As her eyes slowly adjusted to the dark, Rachel realized the cave had become wide and spacious, like a gigantic, empty closet.

Elliot stopped for a moment, leaning against a wall to rest.

"Oh, no," he moaned.

"What? What is it?" Rachel tightened her grip on his jacket. Something horrible was happening. Elliot had seen the Giant Hairy Man who lived in the cave and ate nothing but children. She just knew it.

"My hat . . . it's gone," Elliot moaned again. "I must have lost it when we bellyflopped into this place to avoid becoming dog lunch."

"Your hat?" Rachel's relief that they weren't about to be eaten quickly became a laser beam of anger. She aimed it straight at Elliot. "We're trapped in a bottom-less cave by a man-eating dog, and you're worried about how your head looks?"

"It's my lucky hat. Dad says every time I wear it we make an important archeological find."

"Oh, really?" Rachel dared. "By the time someone finds us in here, *we'll* be fossils."

Elliot didn't respond. Instead he removed his glasses and unzipped his jacket.

"My glasses are fogged over," he said. "Do you find it warm in here?"

"I don't find *anything* in here—it's too dark!"

"Seriously. It feels as if someone cranked up the fur-nace." He wriggled out of his jacket. "And I keep hear-ing this sound . . ."

"Like a rumbling or gurgling?" finished Rachel. The sound had grown louder in the past few minutes.

"Exactly. Up ahead somewhere." He squinted into the dimness. "Looks as if the cave curves to the left. Maybe it leads to another entrance."

It *had* grown warmer inside the cave. As they shuffled

around the cave's curving path, the cold, rocky soil
beneath their feet turned soft and spongy, oozing a
thin sheen of muck that stuck to their shoes. Just
beyond the curve, the footpath narrowed into a passageway. A tiny white reflection glimmered on its rock
wall, like the glow of the moon bouncing from a still
pond.

"Look! There's a light!"

"I see it," grunted Elliot as he rescued his shoe from
a puddle of muck. "Come on."

He shot out ahead into the passage, toward the danc-
ing light. Rachel brought up the rear as quickly as she
could, slipping and sliding past the rocky walls of the
cave. But before she could reach the other side, a spi-
raling curtain of refreshing mist whirled around her.

"Elliot!" Rachel's voice came back to her in a chorus
of echoes, barely perceptible over the loud rush ahead.
She called out again. "Elliot! You had better answer me
or you'll lose more than just that ratty hat of yours!"

A bouncing voice, slightly lower than her own, fun-
neled into her ears.

"Follow my voice!"

Rachel stepped from the passageway toward Elliot's
call. It was like stepping through a doorway into a
warm summer evening. An umbrella of brightening
stars floated overhead, winking down on the bare
plateau where she stood. They were still inside the
mountain, but the cave had opened into an enormous
cavern. Light filtered in through an archlike porthole
along one wall, illuminating the giant room with sunrays
that had passed through yards of centuries-old glacial

ice. To her right, a sheer rock cliff led to a yawning, bottomless ravine. A babbling brook coursed along the floor of the cavern, cascading down a flat bed of stones some distance away until it splashed to its final destination, far below in the gathering darkness of the ravine. For a moment Rachel thought she had ignored Armut's blessing and had fallen off the mountain, into another world.

"Pretty amazing, isn't it?" Elliot called, hopping over a small, steaming water hole near the rushing water. He came to stand beside her.

"What is this place?" Rachel managed to squeak out.

"Don't get all gaga on me now, Rachel. This is Turkey, remember?" Elliot said slowly, as if talking to a two year old. "Gobble gobble. Moun-tain. Big moun-tain. We look for ark on moun-tain."

"But this river. And the waterfalls." Rachel craned her neck upward. Tiny sparkles flashed in the dark, endless space high above them. "And the stars! Look at all the stars! There must be thousands of them!"

"Pyrite," came Elliot's reply.

"Pie-what?"

"You know . . . pyrite. Fool's gold. It's a common mineral. These rocks in the mountain are full of fool's gold. You didn't think you were seeing stars in the middle of the day, did you?"

Rachel's stomach did a flip-flop. Elliot kept talking, but she quit listening. Instead, she heard the words of Old Tuz coming back to her in an instant: *A thousand tiny golden stars twinkled around us, and yet the sun shone upon us, for it was daylight. And there, where night and day meet inside the mountain, was the great ship.*

"Rachel? Rachel? You in there?" The tapping of Elliot's knuckles on top of her skull brought Rachel back to reality. "Your eyes look like glazed doughnuts. We better sit down for a minute." He guided her toward what appeared to be a boxcar-shaped rock bridge protruding from the back cavern wall.

"I'm fine," Rachel mumbled, dragging along behind him. "I was just thinking. About Old Tuz."

"It's a shame he couldn't have come with us," Elliot said as they reached the boxcar bridge. He dropped his jacket, spread it out along the warm stone floor and motioned for her to sit. "He might have enjoyed another visit to this old volcano."

A fine spray of cool mist and the word "volcano" hit Rachel the moment she sat.

"Volcano?"

"Volcano. You're sitting on one. Well, in one, actually. What was it you said Old Tuz called Ararat?" asked Elliot.

Rachel again conjured up the memory of the old man. "The mountain . . . that burns within," she recollected.

"Ararat is just an old, sleeping volcano. Remember that beating heart Armut talked about? It's the lava underneath us." Elliot paced as he thought. "No wonder it's so toasty in this cave. The lava warms the rocks, they radiate heat, the glacier slowly melts to form a river . . ."

"And we're trapped inside a volcano," Rachel finished.

"Lovely." She slumped back against the cavern wall and forced out a sigh, partly from exhaustion and partly out of frustration with their plight. This snooping adventure had quickly become a dangerous one. Even more frightening, Rachel began to feel homesick—a feeling she seldom experienced.

She kicked at a small dark rock half covered by Elliot's jacket. With a hollow sound, it skittered from under the jacket and Elliot bent absentmindedly to pick it up. Suddenly he stood bolt upright. Without a word, he stepped away from Rachel and the cavern wall, his eyes staring above and behind her, his mouth hanging open like a panting bulldog.

"That's a childish trick, Elliot. I look around, there is nothing there, and you say, 'gotcha!' It isn't funny, especially since we're doomed to die in here."

Elliot's expression remained frozen. The dark object Rachel had kicked still lay in the palm of his hand. Slowly his eyes came to rest on hers. A mystical grin soon followed.

"Take a look at this." He tossed her the small object. Remembering the sheep dung incident hours earlier, she pulled back her hands, refusing to catch another of Elliot's gags. It landed with a soft thud on his jacket. Rachel peered between her feet at the irregularly shaped piece of hardened wood. A half circle, carved in the face of the wood and surrounded by lines streaming out from it, peered back at her, like a broken picture-book sun in a cloudless sky. It was identical to the picture etched into Yedi's clay tablet—the matching half to Old Tuz's necklace.

"Now," Elliot said in amazement, pointing through her to a spot on the cavern wall, "take a look at *that*."

Slowly, Rachel rose to her feet, afraid to turn around. She tiptoed toward Elliot and his silly grin. When she had reached a safe distance from the wall, she closed her eyes, spun around, and, after a moment of uncertainty, popped open her eyes. Before her loomed the great boxcar bridge. The hulking mass towered over her and Elliot and, in the icy light of the cavern, she quickly realized that the bridge was not a bridge at all. It was instead a huge rectangle of dark, dense wood, large enough to cover a football field. A ship. An enormous, hollow ship, capable of carrying a cargo of animals in rough seas for months. Rachel knew she was staring into the belly of Noah's ark.

It lay at an angle inside the cavern like a colossal piece of driftwood, jutting from the inner walls of the mountain where it had lodged precariously on the level cliff, just short of an endless drop-off. The rear of the ship remained encased in rock and ice, permanently held in the mountain's strong grasp.

For centuries, the brook had carved a shallow outline around the corner of the great structure, wearing deeper with each summer thaw. Its gurgling waters now encircled the mighty ship with a knee-deep moat of melted ice. Rachel felt as if time itself had melted away, leaving only herself, Elliot, and the ancient ship that had carried all of humanity.

"That old doodlebug wasn't crazy after all," she mumbled aloud. She glanced at Elliot. He stood behind her, facing the ark and adjusting the wire-rimmed glasses on his bewildered face.

After a long, reverent silence, Elliot finally spoke.

"It's enormous. It's gigantic. And look at the hull . . . you can still see the joints and grooves and separate wooden planks. Amazing!" He stepped closer and cocked a critical eye. "Ancient earthquakes and lava flows probably sealed it in this cavern. I'm surprised the glacier didn't shove it over the cliff."

"So?" Rachel said indifferently.

"So? SO! We're gawking at Noah's ark, the REAL Noah's ark, and all you can say is 'So?'"

"So . . . stop analyzing it with that microscopic brain of yours and let's go see where the elephants lived."

Rachel drew a deep breath, then stepped through the broad opening fashioned in the hull, apparently where a large door had once sealed the ark. Elliot nearly toppled her over in his rush to follow.

"It smells like . . . like . . . ," Rachel searched for the proper word. "Christmas."

"Probably the wood," Elliot replied, pressing his hands gingerly against the ship's inner walls. "Gopher wood, remember? It could be cypress wood, although it almost looks like oak of some sort. It's tough to tell—the timbers have really darkened over time."

"This wood doesn't look as if it was chewed by gophers," Rachel pointed out.

They were standing in what seemed to be a pair of large rooms joined by a high ceiling. Many of the wooden planks above were missing. Gaping holes stared down upon them from the two upper decks of the ship. A system of ladders woven throughout the inner hull

provided access to a maze of compartments for food
storage and animal stalls. Some of the ladders were
missing rungs, and some were destroyed completely.
Long wooden pegs held everything together.

The flat floor under their feet held large fenced stalls,
with smaller stable rooms visible through holes in the
higher decks. A drop chute pegged against one wall
caught Elliot's engineering eye.

"That's probably for hay," he pointed out. "Worked just
like a hayloft in a modern-day barn. They could drop
food down for the larger animals as they needed it."

Rachel didn't make a habit of visiting barns, although
the few she had seen at British riding stables looked
much like this one. Except they didn't float.

High above the top deck hung a ring of lights.

"Look up there," Rachel discovered. Those must be
the skylight windows we read about in Uncle Mason's
Bible."

Elliot squinted up. "The light came in, the barn smell
went out. I like it."

For what must have been hours, the pair explored
every stall and every stable of the ark they could reach
by foot or by ladder. Rachel lost all track of time. She
found herself wandering along the deck planks imagin-
ing the sights, the sounds . . . even the smells of the
voyage so long ago. The squared hull, once noisy and
teeming with activity, now stood like a sanctuary, silent
and solemn. *It's like strolling in a giant, empty church,*
Rachel thought. Actually, she went into churches about
as often as she went into barns. But this ark was special. It had a life all its own.

Elliot seemed as interested in the ark's design as he did in its awesome age. He marveled aloud at how the mountain had preserved the ship. Finally he crawled his way through a rotten skylight out onto the top of the ark.

"Rachel! Rachel, I found something!"

"Let me guess—a pair of unicorns loose on deck three?"

"Better than that," he called down. "I found a way out of the cave."

Rachel jogged the length of deck two, climbed yet another ladder, and squeezed through the rotten skylight opening onto a roof of moss, green as a golf course.

"See the passageway?" Elliot asked. Rachel nodded. Above them, a sliver of light curved upward into a hollowed space in the rock where the ark entered the unyielding cavern wall.

"What's that whistling noise?"

"The wind," Elliot answered. "There must be an opening at the end of this tunnel. Come on." Rachel followed him into the passageway up a set of natural stairsteps chiseled into the floor by wind and water. It was an easy climb: up, around several bends, down again, and into a space so small they had to crawl on hands and knees to squeeze through. Finally, the whistling wind led them to the exit Elliot had promised— a fog-white open doorway no bigger than a manhole cover. Out they climbed, one at a time, onto a tilted table of rock nudged against the mountain. A bank of wispy clouds had settled over the slopes since they had begun their journey at sunrise. Fog circled them like smoke from a thousand campfires.

When Elliot wasn't looking, Rachel drew out her Kurdish scarf and placed the smooth nugget of ark wood into it. Carefully she wrapped it, the same way she had wrapped her fragile teacups when she and her mother moved from Great Britain to Kentucky. Then she tucked it back into her pocket. Even through the scarf she could feel a pulsating warmth from the ancient wood.

Elliot blinked slowly at the fog as if his brain had slipped into neutral. He had to be dead tired from those late-night sessions decoding Yedi's tablet. Rachel decided to give his brain a kick start.

"Well, what are you waiting for, Mr. Adventure?" she taunted. "Race you down the mountain!"

In her rush to get a head start, she bolted out onto the damp rock. For a moment, Rachel saw her blurry reflection in the wet, slippery stone that encased the mountain. An instant later, she could see nothing but sky as her feet slid from beneath her. Instinctively she lunged backward, grasping for something to break her fall—which happened to be Elliot. Together they tumbled from the slick rock ledge, Rachel first with Elliot toppling over her. She slammed against the pebbled slope beneath with force enough to knock the wind from her chest. The sound of Elliot's voice calling her name seemed miles away as she skidded down the slope, face up, eyes wide open.

# CHAPTER 12

One jolt, then two. Then a sharp pain shot like fire through her right leg. A freezing numbness soon followed. Slowly Rachel raised her head to peer at the large boulder that had stopped her downhill slide.

Elliot skittered to her side moments later, sporting a fresh scrape along his cheek and a lopsided twist in his glasses.

"Are you okay?" he panted.

"Do I look okay to you?" she snapped, then quickly added an agonizing moan. Slowly she sat up and cradled her ankle in her hands. It felt cold and hot inside, all at the same time. "I've lost feeling in my foot," she whined. "And I think my spine is broken."

Elliot surveyed her injured leg.

"You didn't fall off the mountain, Rachel. You just slid down a footpath. I imagine your spine is fine." He carefully tilted her right foot.

"Yow!" Rachel howled.

Elliot adjusted his bent glasses as best he could. "Your ankle is twisted pretty badly.  Maybe fractured."

He stood for a moment to wipe the blood from his cheek, and made a brisk check of the slope. The spotty fog was lifting rapidly now, like a rising curtain. "It'll be dark in an hour or so. We might make it back to the yaila by then if we really put on the speed. If we can find it, that is."

Rachel stared at him and sat stone still, holding her peace for as long as possible. Then she lashed out.

"Maybe you hadn't noticed, but I've just tumbled halfway down the side of the world and quite probably broken major bones and muscles, *including* my spine. My life could be at stake."

Elliot squatted beside her. "Nothing more painful than a broken muscle," he said, chuckling weakly. "Remind me to give you an anatomy lesson when we get back to the museum."

"*IF* we get back to the museum." Rachel knew he was trying to soothe her pain as well as her pride. He had every right to call her something awful for whopping him on the head when she fell. But he didn't. Elliot never went in for the kill, even when the other person asked for it, as Rachel usually did.

Instead, they watched together as the sun sank through the fog to spread a blanket of light across the mountainside. The shadow of the big boulder beside them cast a long wedge of shade where they sat, allowing the mountain chill to creep in around them. It would have been a beautiful sunset if it weren't for their hopeless situation. They were lost, they were alone, and they were in trouble. A dozen yailas lay scattered below them on the mountainside, each resembling the other right down to their tent arrangements and wool blankets. Any one of them might be Selik's.

"We're in trouble, you know." Rachel finally broke the silence.

"I know," Elliot answered. "Dad and Armut must be worried sick."

"Not that sort of trouble. Real trouble," Rachel exclaimed. "We're sitting on top of a volcano; we don't know where we are. And my ankle—I'm not sure I can walk." She shifted her weight and rubbed her legs briskly. "It's like a fridge behind this boulder. Help me move out into the sunshine." She held out her hand, but Elliot ignored her. He glanced around the boulder. "What are you doing?" Rachel attacked with her British accent. "I'm in need of assistance here!"

"Shhhh!" Elliot shushed her. "Someone's coming." He hunkered down behind the rock and sneaked a second quick peek. "Two men . . . and two horses."

"Finally!" Rachel sighed in relief and rubbed at her oversized ankle. "Our ride home!"

"They could be bushwhackers . . . robbers," warned Elliot. "The mountain is crawling with them. And we're in no position to run away." He pointed to her leg.

Rachel immediately threw down a challenge. "We don't know that they are bush-whammers, or whatever you call them. Why don't you stand up and find out?"

"What do you expect me to say? 'Pardon me, sirs, I'm a lost tourist. After you rob me, would you mind ever so much giving my cousin here a ride back to town?'"

"Well, . . . maybe they're government officials," Rachel hoped aloud.

"Not likely. I don't see uniforms." Suddenly Elliot spun around and hunched his back against the rock, his finger pressed to his lips in a warning hush.

"What is it?" came Rachel's half-whispered reply.

"It's your buddies from the teahouse in Dog Biscuit."

Rachel had to see for herself. She peered around the protective boulder. Even against the glare of the late afternoon sun, the black-and white-pants and whirling turban were unmistakable—Zebra Pants and Towel Head. The gun in Zebra Pants' hand also was unmistakable. Her own gasp startled her.

"What do we do?"

Elliot studied the mountain slope for an instant. "Nothing," he whispered. "We just sit tight and hope they're too lazy to look behind the rocks."

The sound of horse hooves clomping on the crusted volcano's side edged closer. Rachel heard the rustle of saddles as the two dismounted.

A pair of long shadows fell across the slope beside their rocky hideaway. For one tense moment the shadows stretched perilously close. Rachel's heart raced. She held what little breath she could catch and squeezed her eyes tightly shut. Maybe if she couldn't see Zebra Pants and Towel Head, they couldn't see her, either. Then the footsteps stopped abruptly on the opposite side of the rocks, and the two shadows froze less than a meter from Rachel's hidden feet.

The first voice Rachel heard was that of Zebra Pants. He no longer spoke polite English as he had at the teahouse. Instead, he angrily barked out gibberish.

Rachel pointed to her ear and shook her head, silently

telling Elliot she couldn't understand them. He ignored her and squinted in total concentration. The two men continued to jabber at one another. Finally, the long shadow of Zebra Pants' hand pointed toward the mountain summit. The sound of horses' hooves echoed between the mountains. Then the men, the horses, and their shadows all disappeared up the mountain.

"Well, that wasn't exactly a pleasant experience, was it?" Rachel sighed in relief.

Elliot slowly turned to face her.

"They're counting on our getting lost up here . . . and not returning. And if the mountain doesn't do us in . . ." He drew his finger across his throat with one quick, deadly stroke.

" . . . then they will," Rachel finished his sentence. She thought for a moment. "Wait a minute . . . how do you know what they plan to do? That was gibberish they were speaking, not hieroglyphics, or whatever you archeologists speak." Suddenly she remembered the yaila, and how Elliot spoke to the local women.

He shrugged his shoulders.

"So I picked up a little more of the local language than I thought . . ."

Rachel's face still registered disbelief.

"Okay, so I also did some studying at home before we left. . . . Look, the important thing is, they're going to kill us if we don't get out of here. They plan to blame our disappearance on the Turkish army—which means our government won't trust the Turkish government anymore, and the freedom fighters are one step closer to taking over."

So that was the rebels' plan; accuse army officials of kidnapping American tourists. Old Tuz was right again—there *were* snakes on the mountain—two-legged snakes.

"So," she sputtered, swallowing hard, "they really are going to do us in."

"They'll have to catch us first," Elliot said, determinedly. He helped Rachel to her feet. "Can you walk?"

She pressed down lightly on her right foot. Her shin and ankle ached painfully.

"No!" she yelped.

"Well, here's a news flash for you," Elliot said in his firmest voice. "If you can't walk, they'll catch us. And if they catch us . . ."

"Alright, alright!"

He took her by the arm and guided her down a flat open slope in the opposite direction from the rebels. With every step, Rachel groaned and favored her right leg. She leaned hard on Elliot's shoulder with her arm, and after only fifty meters of limp-hopping down the stony slope, Rachel knew they would never make it down to the yaila, to *any* yaila, before nightfall.

"I have to stop," she finally sighed. "My foot is getting numb."

Elliot guided her to a smooth area in the center of a boulder field just above a small ridge and slowly lowered her to the ground, her sore leg sticking out in front of her.

"Help me get my shoe off," she told him.

"Nope. You've got to leave it on," he said, shaking his head. "If you don't, your ankle will swell up like a cantaloupe." He reached under her arms and with one hard pull he yanked her to her feet. "We've got to keep moving, Rachel. In another hour . . . ," Elliot's voice trailed off. He cocked his head to one side, then shot a quick look toward the ridge below them. Rachel opened her mouth to retort when an all-too-familiar sound clicked across the boulder field from below the ridge. Horse hooves.

They couldn't run. There was nowhere to hide. They would have to face the rebels here on the slope of Mount Ararat, alone. Rachel found herself standing tall, despite her injured foot. One hand was clenched into a hard, determined fist. The other clutched the chunk of wood in her pocket. She imagined the headline in the newspapers back home: "Two Missing in Turkish Mountain Mishap. Local Girl Disappears Without a Trace."

A voice called out and the sound of hooves stopped abruptly. Elliot stepped in front of Rachel, placing himself between her and the sound of the animals. A small pair of olive-skinned hands reached over the ridge of rock, followed by a swirling blue turban and a thin, wiry body draped in an oversized sweater. Rachel's tight fist uncurled at the sight of the dark eyes shining from beneath the turban.

"Yedi!"

"We do not have much time," Yedi said in a half-whisper. "Please come. Quickly." Without another word, Yedi edged his shoulder under Rachel's arm for support and moved her toward the ridge. Elliot lifted her other arm and did likewise.

"But what . . . how did you find us? How did you get here?" Rachel sputtered.

No sooner had they reached the edge of the ridge than Rachel's question was answered. Two meters below them on a faded pathway stood the donkey cart from Selik's yaila—complete with two small, strong-willed donkeys hitched in front. A broad smile burst across Elliot's face.

"Cinderella," he said to Rachel, "your carriage awaits."

With a little maneuvering, the pair managed to lower Rachel past the lip of the ridge down onto the hard wooden seat just behind the two donkeys. Yedi bounded into the driver's seat next to her while Elliot scrambled into the open bed of the two-wheeled cart atop a lumpy pile of wool blankets. With a few short clicks of Yedi's tongue, the cart jerked into motion under full donkeypower, lurching back and forth like a cockeyed rocking chair. A faint trail leading down the mountain seemed to appear magically beneath each plodding step of the donkeys.

"Yedi," Elliot finally began, as he tossed a blanket around Rachel's shoulders and buried himself in the remaining pile. "Yedi, we found it."

Yedi remained silent. An understanding smile hung on his face, shaped like the crescent moon that had risen above them in the spreading sunset. Then he spoke.

"Yes. I know."

"What do you mean, you *know*?" Rachel launched. "How would you know that?" She fumed hotter with each bumpy jolt of the donkey cart. "You've been following us, haven't you?" She twisted her neck to peer at Elliot. "Did you hear him? He's been here all along, watching us become sheepdog pie . . . probably saw me fall and almost break my precious neck!" She twisted back to face Yedi. "If you know where we've been, then you know we were nearly kidnapped by the Turkey twins!"

"Uh . . . Rachel," Elliot reasoned. "Two things. Number one, pipe down. Half of Asia can hear you out here, including Zebra Pants and his buddy with the beach blanket wrapped around his skull. And number two . . ." He leaned forward, pressed his face between her and Yedi, and whispered softly. "You're hollering at the brave Kurd who has just saved your skin from Turkish rebels. I'd thank him if I were you."

Yedi seemed to understand that thanks and apologies from Rachel were as rare as four-leaf clovers, and that he would be lucky to get either one. His gaze remained fixed ahead.

"We are not yet safe," he said. "With the darkness, the rebels will come back from the mountain. Their horses are like the wind against this cart and these donkeys."

Yedi guided the creaky cart as it lumbered on toward smoother slopes. As the sun disappeared, the cool evening breeze began to rattle the canvas shells of tents clustered into yailas along the horizon.

After a time, Elliot spoke up.

"How did you know we had found the ark?"

"You are changed," Yedi replied. "Each one who has been to the great ship wears a glow beneath the skin.

It cannot be hidden, even in this one." He nodded at Rachel.

She shook her head in disgust. "The only glow I see is the one from inside your brain from too many of your uncle's campfire stories." The pain in her ankle had faded to a dull throb, just enough to make her crankier than usual. She slumped against the hard wooden seat with a heavy sigh. "And the only glow I care to see right now is the one from that same silly campfire." She paused in the dim light, then added, "I never thought I'd hear myself say that."

"Hey, you wanted adventure, right? Well, 'we deliver.'" Even with that scrape on his cheek, Elliot was practically his chipper old self again. Which made Rachel ill. She thought of a wonderful comeback that compared Elliot to the two headstrong animals pulling their cart, but she never got the chance to share it. Yedi reached out with his thin hand to signal silence and slowly eased the cart off the path into the cover of some large boulders.

"What's the matter? Did your donkeys run out of gas or something?" Rachel quipped.

Yedi held a finger to her lips and looked earnestly in her eyes. "The rebels have returned from the mountain." His voice was calm but firm.

"That's it, isn't it?" Elliot thought aloud. "You stayed behind this morning in case we ran into trouble. Zebra Face and his bath-towel sidekick have been on our trail all day long, and you've been shadowing them in this rickety cart. They probably thought you were just some old shepherd joyriding around the mountain."

"I am a shepherd," replied Yedi, with a grin in his voice. "But I am not an old shepherd."

Yedi had fooled everyone, including Rachel. Broken ankle or not, she smiled to herself at his spunk. He really had saved their skins. So she gave him one of her rare compliments.

"You sneaky old snoop."

## CHAPTER 13

With the mountain behind them and the dig somewhere ahead, Yedi tugged the reins and steered their
cart off the faint path and into the rough countryside
surrounding them. They followed a wide, looping arch
through jagged terrain for at least twenty minutes.
Finally, the darkness and her own impatience overpow-
ered Rachel.

"Wait a minute," she challenged him. "Isn't the dig in
the other direction?"

Yedi focused on the new path he had chosen. "Yes."
He pulled a tighter rein on the donkeys.

Her earlier compliment was forgotten. "That turban
of yours has cut off the air supply to your brain!" She
pointed to the donkeys. "See? Even they know we're
going the wrong way."

Her comments went unanswered. Yedi snapped the
reins and picked up the pace a bit. They had reached a
dirt road now, one crisscrossed by dusty trails of animal carts and sandals. He urged the donkeys onto it,
and immediately Rachel felt the cart tilt backward

against the road's steep grade. In fact, Elliot and his pile of blankets slid to the rear of the wagon bed, rousing him from a long-overdue rest. Elliot reached behind his glasses, rubbed his eyes for a moment, and glanced up at the faint stars for guidance.

"Where are we headed, Yedi? The dig's over that way."

"Maybe you can talk some sense into him—I certainly can't," Rachel chimed in. Her voice jiggled as the cart tilted side to side with each rut in the worn road.

The climb grew steeper stil, and a sharp turn suddenly brought them face-to-face with a massive wall just ahead. Against the night sky, Rachel could make out the silhouette of what appeared to be a tall rocket ship towering over a gigantic Hershey's Kiss.

"Goodness Agnes!" came Elliot's hushed voice. "The Ishak Pasha Saray Palace. I never dreamed it was so big."

"That old palace we nearly crashed into with that trash-heap airplane?" Rachel snapped. "What are we doing here? Dropping in for evening tea?"

The road leveled onto a raised terrace overlooking the valley below, where the dig lay, protected by the timeless chain of mountains. A wall of stone extended in both directions along the terrace ridge, and a wide gateway with intricate carvings beckoned to them to enter a yawning courtyard just inside. Yedi barely slowed down as they passed through the gateway. As they entered, Rachel heard the muffled pounding of horse hooves in the dark distance.

Elliot cocked his ear to one side. "Zebra Pants?"

Yedi nodded his silent reply and aimed the donkey cart straight through another arched portal, this one even fancier than the first. It led them into a large inner courtyard. To their left lay the remains of storehouses that once held grain and other supplies. To the right, another portal led to an open-air reception room where the pasha, the palace ruler, held audience with his subjects long ago. Rachel recognized it all thanks to Elliot's vivid descriptions of the place. He'd never been there, of course, but like everything else, he had read all about it.

Straight ahead, a twisting maze of rooms faded into the darkness. Yedi pulled up to the maze entrance and motioned for Elliot and Rachel to go in. The sting in Rachel's ankle had eased a bit, so she limped down from the cart unaided and followed Elliot into the first room. A few of the rooms still had ceilings although most along the outer wall were open. Anyone willing to scale the wall could easily climb out . . . or in.

They listened as Yedi drove the donkeys to the storehouse area of the courtyard. Soon he joined them.

"The rebels will look for us here," he said. "We must not be found."

"Brilliant deduction, Sherlock," Rachel said. "So how do you propose we stop them?"

"I've got an idea," Elliot piped up. "If we stay near these inside rooms, away from the outer wall, they can't look down from above and see us. Maybe we can lose them in the palace. Just like Cat and Mouse or Hide-and-Seek." He swallowed. "Only without a base." He glanced in Rachel's direction. "Can you make it?"

A voice beyond the outer wall halted Rachel's answer. Zebra Pants and Towel Head had arrived, and from the sound of it, they had already passed through the first courtyard.

Elliot led the way, stepping into the confusion of rooms. Rachel shuffled behind with Yedi following. The plan was a simple one: move quietly into a room, crouch in the corner, listen for the rebels, then decide where to go next. It would work for awhile, but sooner or later they would run out of rooms. And time.

The rebels gained a quick advantage by scaling the wall as Elliot had predicted. Rachel couldn't see them, but she tracked their location by their sharp exchanges in gibberish. By using the wall, they had narrowed their hot pursuit to the few inner rooms. Cat and Mouse had now become Cat and Trapped Rats. She stared into the dimness at Elliot, who could only shrug his shoulders as if to say, "Well, they've outsmarted us this time. Time to think of something else."

Though the future seemed as dim as the night around them, Rachel just couldn't give up hope. Not yet. After all, they had found the ark, touched it with their own hands, walked where the grand old man Noah had fed the elephants. She thrust her hand into her pocket and grabbed at the scarf. A reassuring lump of wood filled her fist and she knew, then and there, that even rebel Kurds were no match for Yedi's snoopiness, Elliot's courage and smarts, and Noah's God.

Yedi took the lead and gestured for them to follow. Cutting through several open passages, he led them bravely across the floor of a large feast room near the center of the maze and into more interconnected rooms on the other side. A patchwork of portals, each with its own mirror, lined the feast room walls. According to Elliot, the Walking Turkish Encyclopedia, this feast room was a hit with tourists, because the pasha had designed the mirrors so that feasts could be observed from the rooms next door, but not the other way around. That way the pasha's family could see the feasts from the maze of rooms but remain hidden from view, as custom required.

Yedi leaned over and whispered something in Elliot's ear. Moments later, he vanished. Elliot directed Rachel to one corner of their new maze room. Halfway down the wall stood a mirror anchored to an arched door-way, providing a superb view into the feast room in the dim light. Then Elliot took a position opposite her where he, too, had a clear view of a mirror and the feast room.

A striped image flashed before Rachel in her mirror. From the safety of her corner perch she watched Zebra Pants slink through the feast room. He couldn't see her, of course—the pasha and his mirrors had fixed that problem over a hundred years ago. But she could sure see him.

As Zebra Pants slunk about, Elliot and Rachel shifted their view to the next appropriate mirror, following his every move. *This is snooping at its finest,* Rachel thought. *Too bad Yedi is missing out.* They watched and waited . . . watched and waited. Finally Towel Head moved into view. The rebels whispered to one another, then both exited the feast room through a portal on the far wall, away from Rachel's hiding spot.

She watched as Elliot edged his way past one doorway, then another, like a lioness stalking her prey. He didn't take his eyes off the feast room until he reached Rachel's side.

"We've got one chance," he whispered. "Quick!" He helped Rachel limp under an archway, across the feast room floor, and out the doorway that led back to the palace storehouse chamber. But there was no cart, there were no donkeys. No Yedi. Together they ducked into the reception room just off the storehouse courtyard. The roof here, if there ever was one, had crumbled away long ago, leaving only the dark sky and crescent moon above them. They huddled silently against the inner wall, out of view from the archway, for several long minutes. It was a guessing game now. He who guessed best guessed last.

"Where is that blasted Yedi?" Rachel whispered at last. "He said he would be right behind us."

Elliot seemed to be sizing up a series of doors lining one wall. He turned to her and, in the faint starlight, Rachel swore she detected a smile.

"He's hiding the donkeys. You're worried about him, aren't you?"

She shifted uncomfortably, but not because of her ankle. This was one of those times when Elliot seemed to read her mind.

"Worried? About that yaila yo-yo? I should think not. My only worry is that he has abandoned us in this rat's maze of a palace, and now we're trapped. Just like rats."

"I'm worried about him too," replied Elliot, ignoring her remark. "But I get the feeling he's got something up his sleeve—or under his turban, I mean."

"Too bad it's not a brain."

*Whap!*

A stinging slap rang out just beyond the archway. The grinding sound of donkey hooves and cart wheels followed a split second later. Rachel went numb as she listened to their only means of escape clatter away from the palace. The fleeing donkey cart meant one of two things: either Yedi had run away—without them— or the rebels had captured him, in which case it was now one down, and two to go. She gulped.

Elliot grabbed her arm and broached a third possibility, one she had been afraid to consider.

"I don't believe it," Elliot murmured into the starry sky. "You know what Yedi's doing, don't you? He's riding that clacking cart back to the mountain. The rebels are sure to follow him, thinking it's all of us. He's set himself up as a decoy."

Yedi knew the rebels better than anyone, and he certainly knew what terrible deeds they were capable of. The very idea that he would lure them away using himself as bait flabbergasted Rachel. It also made her feel small. Was this the plan he had tucked into that turban of his?

Sure enough, two horses soon trotted by outside. Zebra Pants growled orders in gibberish, then both rebels zipped away on their mounts toward the mountain. Even with a head start, the donkey cart was no match for rebel horses. Yedi said so himself. In ten minutes tops, they would overtake the cart and do who-knows-what before returning to the palace to claim two trapped rats.

"We should never have let him stay out there alone," Elliot said of Yedi.

Immediately Rachel recalled every rude remark she had made to Yedi. Now it was too late to take each one back. She had made plans to explore this old palace from day one, thinking it might be where her adventures would begin during this week of forced camp life. Instead, it looked as if her adventure would end here. Permanently. She imagined Armut and Uncle Mason waiting anxiously at the dig site, pacing back and forth. She thought of Selik at the yaila, wondering, as he watered their horses, why they had not returned. It all seemed so real to Rachel that she could almost hear the familiar tinkle of bells on Yedi's saddle, like a faraway voice singing on the night breeze.

Wait a minute . . . there! She heard it again—the sound of the snoopy Santa Claus bells. Elliot must have heard it too, for he stiffened and grew dead still. A fourth possibility suddenly leaped into her brain. The donkeys and the cart were gone. But that didn't mean the donkey *driver* was gone. Now it was Rachel's turn to smile in the starlight.

"Ohhhh . . . ," she cooed. "That sly sneak. Decoy indeed." She struggled to her feet and hobbled to the middle door on the opposite wall. Startled, Elliot sprang up, but Rachel had already lifted the latch. With one hard yank she jerked open the door, only to find two Kurdish faces staring in—Yedi and his horse.

"I thought we'd lost you! To rebels!" Elliot burst out.

"Oh, I could never be lost in these mountains. Not even in the dark," he replied with a grin.

Without thinking, Rachel hugged him around the neck. Then, coming to her senses, she hobbled back, cleared her throat and said, "You've broken Ground Rule One, you know, straying off on your own like that!"

Yedi seemed puzzled. "Why do you have rules about the ground?"

"Look, you two," Elliot broke in. "This is one lovely conversation, but you can have it somewhere else. Right now we've got ten minutes to find our way out of here and get gone. After that, we're Kurdish rebel stew."

"This way." Yedi backed his horse from the reception room and helped Elliot boost Rachel into the saddle. They passed through several long rooms, Yedi leading his mare, and Elliot walking behind, before reaching a weathered hole in the tall outer wall.

"The dig lies there," stated Yedi, pointing down an easy incline.

"Wait!" honked Rachel. She unhooked the saddle bells and plopped them into a side pouch near the stirrup, where they fell completely silent. "There." She glared down at her two companions. "*Now* you may go."

"Yes, Effendi," teased Yedi.

Elliot clicked to the horse. "You heard the Young Wise One. Let's roll."

**CHAPTER 14**

"But the donkeys!" Rachel exclaimed. "What about the donkeys?" She pulled her blanket tightly around herself and drew another long sip from her cup of hot tea.

Yedi stared into the kerosene lamplight filling the warm tent. The familiar sights and sounds of the dig site around them were real this time, not just imagined. It felt good to be home, even when home was a tent, a campfire, and a jolly, pear-shaped Kurd. Armut's round face glowed like a smiling full moon hanging above Yedi's cot. The shuffling feet circling the campfire outside the tent belonged to Uncle Mason. Everyone at the dig, even the workers, were waiting to hear about their adventure and harrowing escape from the rebels.

There was the small matter to clear up with Uncle Mason and Armut of course, including a full explanation of how and why Yedi, Elliot, and Rachel came to be on the mountain alone in the first place. Indeed, their arrival back here at the dig an hour ago had been a mixture of joyous relief followed by a stern lecture.

Rachel recalled hearing Ground Rules One and Three mentioned several times. But before the story of their adventure could be told, Rachel had to know what had happened to the missing donkey cart.

"Well? The donkeys?" she pressed.

"They are quite safe," said Yedi. "The donkeys belong to Selik. Their home is the yaila. So I sent them home with the cart, where they belong. Like me, a donkey cannot be lost in the mountains." He smiled. "They are wise animals."

"Right," Elliot laughed. He flipped over on his cot and adjusted the wire-rims above his bandaged cheek. "Stubborn, yes. Wise . . . well . . ."

"Wisdom comes in many forms," Yedi reminded him. Rachel wasn't sure she liked the way Yedi nodded at her when he talked about wisdom. And donkeys.

Uncle Mason popped his head through the drawn curtain of the tent. "Uh, speaking of wise," came his booming voice, "there is someone here to see . . . the Young Wise One?"

"That would be Rachel," said Elliot.

A ragged, stooped form of a man entered the tent, guided by two Kurdish locals. A hush fell over everyone present, even the workers. They watched as the old man's swollen knuckles reached out to find a stool and, with the deliberate motions of one who cannot see, he sat down slowly. Rachel uncurled her blanket and set her cup aside. Here, in the lamplight, Old Tuz looked more like a grandfather than the jabbering lunatic she had seen at the teahouse.

After an uncomfortable silence, Rachel spoke first.

"You have come to see me?" she inquired.

"You have seen the great ship," he said. He wasn't asking. Instead, he was confirming what he already knew. Rachel moved closer to the old Kurd. She didn't need to answer—Old Tuz nodded her reply for her.

Carefully, she tugged at the leather strap around his neck. "Your wooden amulet," she began in her most polite British accent. "May I see it?"

Old Tuz lowered his bowed neck and removed the necklace. The amulet dangled from his crooked hands, its shadow swaying gently across the tent canvas like the pendulum of an old-fashioned clock.

"There," she went on. "Hold it right there a moment." She pulled her jacket from beneath the cot and took the colorful Kurdish scarf from the pocket. Tugging first one corner, then another, Rachel revealed the nugget of time-polished wood at its center.

Armut gasped quietly. Uncle Mason moved in for a closer look, his brow wrinkled with curiosity. Taking Old Tuz's hands in hers, Rachel lifted the amulet higher. The boatlike etching and partial sun carved upon the necklace stood out in the lamplight.

"Now," she said aloud to herself, "if I can just . . . match up . . . the proper . . ." She twisted her nugget next to the amulet. Finally her puzzle piece of wood locked into that of Old Tuz's. The etchings on Rachel's wood chunk fit perfectly into the necklace, adding the missing rays of sunlight to the carved sun and completing the broken bow of the ship image.

Elliot couldn't stay on his cot. He scrambled to the worktable and sorted through his muddle of papers until he spied the burnished metal chest. Its jeweled lid opened at his touch. Inside lay the ancient clay tablet that had launched this whole crusade.

He carried the chest to Uncle Mason, who had already put his spectacles on for a closer look. Elliot calmly pointed to the squiggly symbols near the tablet's end, the same symbols etched into the ark wood. Uncle Mason's lips parted. "Goodness . . ."

"Agnes!" finished Armut. "It is The Cradle of my people. You have been to the great ship on the Mountain of Nu-Wah!"

"It was just as you told us," Rachel said into Old Tuz's milky eyes. "The golden stars, the icy river, the warm stones . . ."

"Yes, yes," the old man nodded.

"Pyrite, Dad," Elliot explained. "A humongous cavern speckled with fool's gold, like a thousand stars. A wild sheepdog chased Rachel—well, chased *us*—into a cave. I lost my hat . . ." He paused to slap his palm against a cot. "My hat! We never did find it. Anyway, with all the heat from the volcanic stones, part of the glacier had melted inside the cave, and . . ."

Suddenly the whole story came spilling out, Rachel and Elliot together, with Yedi adding the donkey cart play-by-play. Rachel milked her ankle injury for all it was worth and made certain she got plenty of sympathy. There were tales of striped baggy pants, whistling winds, goat yogurt, man-eating dogs, palaces and mirrors. None, however, came close to the *real* adventure of actually finding the ark.

By the time the story was told, the campfire outside

had turned to coals. Rachel had answered a hundred questions. But one question remained unasked.

"Elliot . . . the cave, the cavern—could you find it again?" Uncle Mason asked the question not as a father to a son, but as one archeologist to another. Rachel saw the pride of their ark discovery rush into Elliot's face, but she shared the obvious wave of disappointment that soon followed. Finding the ark the first time was pure luck—if you could call nearly losing your arms and legs to a snarling mountain dog "luck," that is. A second expedition beyond the yaila might lead them to that narrow slit hidden in the mountain where the ark lay. Then again, it might lead them to something less fortunate. Like frostbite, or freedom fighters. But Elliot wasn't one to give up easily.

"I'm not sure," he answered Uncle Mason. "But we could try." Rachel saw the mishmash of cogs and wheels turning in Elliot's brain.

"You still have your map. Yedi has the clay tablet." Uncle Mason removed his spectacles and wiggled them thoughtfully into his shirt pocket. "I believe it's worth another try. But not this time around." He forced a smile. "I'm afraid we've had to change our schedule a bit. Mehlat will be here tomorrow to fly us out. It's too late to petition the Turkish government for more time on such short notice."

"Surely it isn't too late!" Rachel wailed. "If we water the horses now, we can leave in just a few hours. That would put us well up the mountain by sunrise, and—"

"Listen to you. You can barely walk and here you are clamoring to go mountain climbing." As usual, Elliot caught her in an awkward moment. Almost a week ago she would have done anything to escape this place. Now she was fighting to stay on.

"I'll just have to be satisfied with knowing the ark is there. And with the artifact," said Uncle Mason wistfully. He borrowed Rachel's wooden nugget from Old Tuz's fingers and turned it in his own. Then he looked up at Rachel. "This truly is quite a find. The museum in Van will display it in a special way, maybe open a new room—an ark room, perhaps."

"Van! Why the museum in Van? You've got your own museum—a bit shabby with all the poorly wired glass boxes and all, but—"

"Display cases," corrected Elliot.

"Oh, I can call them anything I want if I put my wood in them!" Rachel snapped. "And it *is* my wood, you know. I found it. With my foot."

"It's not exactly yours," Elliot reminded her. "All of the artifacts belong to the people of Turkey, remember? They stay here, with the government."

"But how will we know they're safe?" she asked. "What if the rebels come and whisk them away?"

Uncle Mason smiled. "You're beginning to sound like a real archeologist, Rachel."

Suddenly Old Tuz stood among them. He spoke clearly, with authority.

"I have lived in the mountains all of my years, as did my father and his father. Since long ago the great ship has rested in the land of our people, hidden by the hand of God." He switched the two-piece necklace from one hand to another. "This necklace is not a treasure buried in the ground. It is a gift from my father to me." Nodding slowly, he turned in Rachel's direction. "And now it is my gift . . . to you, Young Wise One. Take it."

"You mean it? It's mine? I can take the wood?" She glanced at Uncle Mason. " . . . to the museum, of course. To SIMA," she hastily added. "We'll open up a room of our own at SIMA. How does 'The Rachel Ashton Artifact Room' sound?"

"Like a room full of dusty glass boxes," surrendered Elliot.

Rachel lifted her nose in the air. "In *my* room we call them 'display cases.'"

### EPILOGUE

"You've got jet lag, Rachel," Elliot said calmly. "When you've zipped through as many time zones as we've crossed in the past two days, you get jet lag. No wonder we're all a little cranky."

"I am *not* cranky!" she snapped. "I'm perfectly fine. I've flown across oceans before and my legs have always worked quite well afterward, thank you. I do not have jet leg."

A faint tapping at the door of Uncle Mason's office brought their argument to a halt—and just when Rachel felt she was winning, too. Arlene, Uncle Mason's secretary, appeared in the doorway with a handful of papers. She was a pleasant, efficient woman, with thick gray hair and steel-gray eyes as sharp as a hawk's hidden behind her silver reading glasses. And she could practically work wonders with Uncle Mason. Rachel had known her for only a few weeks; still, she thought of her as the grandmother she'd never really had.

Arlene had taken care of Uncle Mason's affairs while he was in Turkey, and now that they had returned to Indiana, she was ready to put him to work again. She handed the stack of papers to Uncle Mason.

"You mustn't neglect this work any longer," she said in her kind but firm tone. "The main campus has called twice about artifacts. There is a phone message from Dr. Lane at the Angel Mounds dig at Evansville. And the museum in Van express-mailed a letter." Uncle Mason nodded like a schoolboy who had just received his assignments.

She had barely slipped out the door before she leaned back into the office.

"Oh, and your mother called, dearie," she said to Rachel.

"She called? What did she say? She's supposed to pick me up this afternoon, you know."

"Don't hold your breath, dearie. She said she couldn't make it today. Something about a client or an account or some such thing. It might be as late as Saturday before she arrives." Arlene scooted out the door.

*Saturday?* Rachel had counted on spending the evening in her own room with her own things. Like a bathtub. She should have known better.

"Arlene!" Rachel hollered through the door. "Did you tell Mother we found Noah's ark?"

Arlene's hair and glasses reappeared. "Yes, dearie."

"Well? What did she say?"

Arlene pulled a pink phone message pad from her skirt pocket and held it up to the scrutiny of her silver glasses. "She said . . ." She squinted at the message.

"She said, 'That's nice. See you Saturday.'"

Rachel felt a slow boil rumbling in her stomach. Apparently, Elliot noticed it as well because he quickly made a suggestion.

"Let's go have another look at the display. In the Rachel Ashton Room," he added with a laugh.

She followed him out of the office and through the SIMA workroom, which was messier than ever. They had barely begun the task of unpacking. The travel trunks brimmed over with tools, equipment, and field notebooks. But Uncle Mason made sure the ark wood was the first item unloaded and added to the SIMA collection, along with the Kurdish scarf and Old Tuz's leather strap. He had cleaned up a small, fancy glass case, hooked up a soft light inside it, and cleared away one of those disgusting skeletons to make room for the artifact in a prominent section of the museum.

Elliot led Rachel into the central display room and flipped a light switch hooked to the ark case. A bluish light flickered on, illuminating the two polished wood nuggets, suspended by tiny wires next to one another like cracked puzzle pieces. The leather strap lay curled atop the colorful scarf on the case floor, just as Rachel had arranged them.

"Looks good, Rachel. You did a nice job. Maybe Dad will hire you."

She gazed at the temporary specimen label next to the display. It read: "Wood fragments collected from the vessel known as the ark of Noah, slopes of Greater Ararat, eastern Turkey." Then, in smaller print it read: "On loan from owner/collector, R. Ashton."

"Do you suppose people will believe these really came from Noah's ark?" Rachel asked.

Elliot shrugged his shoulders. "Maybe. Dad's writing up the results of our expedition for a scientific journal so archeologists everywhere will read about our find. *We* know where they came from, though. That's what really counts."

"I suppose so." Rachel sighed and, resting her chin in her palms, she leaned on her elbows beside the display case. She wondered what Yedi and Armut were doing right now. Probably having late-night tea in Dog Biscuit.

A kind, firm voice broke Rachel's trance. Arlene again.

"Oh, I almost forgot," she said. She laid a cardboard box wrapped in brown paper on the table next to Elliot. "This arrived this morning, special delivery."

"Thanks, Arlene." Elliot turned the box slowly on the table.

Rachel peeked at the postmark and saw it was mailed from Dog Biscuit. "Well? Aren't you going to open it?" she pressed.

"I'll open it later. I need to give Dad a hand with unloading the travel trunks."

"You're disgusting," Rachel bounced back. She grabbed the box and stripped the wrapping before Elliot could object. Together they flipped open the box lid.

"Hey! My hat! My lucky hat!" Elliot exclaimed.

"There's a note attached," Rachel observed. She pulled a slip of folded paper from inside the hat brim. "It's from Yedi."

"'Dear Elliot,' " she read aloud. "'Selik found this hat at the yaila. A wild sheepdog dropped it by his campfire. I believe it is yours. Yedi.'"

Elliot lifted the hat to his head and pulled it snug. Then he smiled brim to brim. It looked a little rough around the edges, and two small holes forever marked the spot where the mad dog had clamped his angry teeth into it.

"See?" Elliot shrugged. "I told you it was my lucky hat. How does it look?"

"Ratty as ever. Maybe worse."

He adjusted his glasses and slipped into the workroom to find a mirror.

"Right. Go on, then," she called after him. "Just don't injure yourself kissing the mirror." She sighed dramatically, making certain Elliot could hear. Then she took one last look at the glowing ark display. For an instant she was back on Mount Ararat in the belly of the volcano. The smiling face of Old Tuz appeared in her head.

Absentmindedly, she rummaged through the packing material left in Elliot's hat box, only to find something soft and squishy at the bottom. A quick inspection revealed a fine white tea bag with a note attached.

"What's this?" she uttered aloud. Then she silently read the handwritten message.

"Rachel: Apo Armut has a saying: Wisdom is like tea—both are best when shared with friends. Yedi."

"Rachel?" Elliot stepped from the workroom. "Did you say something?"

"Uh . . . no. I just realized it's nearly time for afternoon tea." She paused. "Would you care to join me?"

"Sure, I guess so." He seemed bewildered by her offer.

"Tea and wisdom are a lot alike, you know," she said, holding up the tea bag while hiding Yedi's note in her fingers. "They should both be shared."

Elliot chuckled and shook his head. "Old Tuz was right. You really are wise."

Rachel just smiled and tucked Yedi's note into her pocket.

## THE END

# The

of the

This story is entirely fictional. Noah's ark has not yet been found. But the Bible states that it came to rest on the mountains of Ararat, which really exist in the country of Turkey. Kurdish people like Yedi, Armut, and Selik live there. Many expeditions have searched for Noah's ark on Greater and Lesser Ararat; you can read more about them in these books:

*The Lost Ship of Noah.* C. Berlitz. New York: G.P. Putnam's Sons, 1987, 203 pages.

*The Quest for Noah's Ark.* J. W. Montgomery. Minneapolis: Bethany Fellowship, Inc., 1972, 335 pages.

*The Ark File.* R. Noorbergen. Mountain View, Calif.: Pacific Press Publishers, 1974, 207 pages.